Adult Entertainment

Short Fiction by
John Metcalf

Macmillan of Canada
A Division of Canada Publishing Corporation
Toronto, Ontario, Canada

Canadian Cataloguing in Publication Data

Metcalf, John, 1938 –
    Adult entertainment

ISBN 0-7715-9896-3

I. Title.

PS8576.E82A78 1986   C813'.54   C86-093808-5
PR9199.3.M47A78 1986

"Single Gents Only" and "Travelling Northward"
have been published previously in the *Malahat Review*.
"The Eastmill Reception Centre" has appeared in
Fiddlehead Magazine.
    Portions of "Polly Ongle", "Single Gents Only",
and "Travelling Northward" have been heard on
CBC- Radio's *Anthology*.

Design: Craig Allen
Author photograph on jacket, copyright 1985,
Peter Milroy, all rights reserved.

Macmillan of Canada
A Division of Canada Publishing Corporation
Toronto, Ontario, Canada

*T*his book is for
Leon and Connie Rooke

Contents

Contents

Polly Ongle

P aul Denton's morning erection was thrusting the sheet into a comic tent. He regarded this sheeted protuberance with resigned pleasure. In one of those manuals which he somehow always found himself ashamedly scanning in bookstores, it had stated that REM sleep was accompanied by erections in males and by engorgement of the labia in females. He thought about that; he thought about engorged labia. He felt generally engorged most of the time but summers were more engorged than winters. He had thought when younger that sexual desire would diminish with age but now, his forty-sixth birthday approaching, he found it was getting worse.

The day's heat was already building.

He felt swept as if on tides of sap, febrile, almost deranged.

Visible in the corner of the window, a great, still spread of maple leaves. In front of the window, the hanging plant's soft tendrils were already brushing the Victorian balloon-back chair. At the back of the house, the small garden plot was teeming with a matto grosso of zucchini and cucumber, stiff hairy stems and open-mouthed flowers. The tomato plants were heavy with green clusters. The tight skin of the green tomatoes, their chaste shine, the hints of white and yellow beneath the green as though they were somehow lighted from within promising a warmth and swelling, made him think of firm, girlish breasts...

Beneath the sheet, he worked his ankle. The pain was quite

1

severe. His laboured jogging along the canal would be impossible for a few days until the shin splints abated, which was probably just as well because it would spare him the torture of having to observe the bob of breasts, cotton shorts wedged in buttock clefts, nipples standing against sweaty T-shirts.

Though the word 'bob' hardly summed the matter up. Some, simultaneously with the 'bob', seemed to *shimmy*, a tremor of flesh which suggested, regardless of size, such confined amplitude, such richness, that it made him want to whimper.

He cranked his ankle harder to see if the pain would dispel, or at least control, the summer riot in his mind of breast, thigh, cleavage, pubic mounds etched by cotton shorts or wind-tautened skirts.

From three floors below rose the voices of Martha and Jennifer.

But what's so bad about goldfish?

Because white cords come out of them and it makes me sick and who has to flush them down the toilet?

What white cords? What are white cords? What...

The front door closed on the voices.

He regretted, daily, having been swayed by the mad enthusiasms of the renovator; he regretted, daily, the very idea of open-plan architecture. The restless night-turnings of his children, the blurts of sleeptalking, the coughs, the soft padding of bare feet on cushioned carpet, the rubber seal on the refrigerator door meeting rubber seal with a *plup*—from his bedroom eyrie in what had been the attic, he could have heard a mouse break wind.

It was open-plan design which he blamed, in part, for the impoverishment of his sex-life. Martha felt uncomfortable, unable to relax if the children were still awake or restless. They used the word 'children' to refer to Alan and Jennifer who were eleven and eight. Peter at fifteen had passed beyond being thought a child by either of them and especially so by Paul.

It seemed to Paul that whenever he was gripped by sexual desire, which was very often, his desires were thwarted by Martha's worrying that the children would hear, would interrupt, that Peter, who was inevitably out, would come in, that the phone might ring, a phone that could not be taken off the hook because Peter, who was out, might have been run over by a truck or fallen into the river or been entrapped by white-slavers. Experience had taught him the futility of attempting to counter these anxieties with reasoned argument; it was futile to point out that Peter had been crossing roads unaided for ten years, that there were no open bodies of water within miles of the movie theatre in which he was seated, that only the most desperate of Arab potentates could lust after a boy with an obnoxious mouth and purple hair.

Nor were the prospects any brighter if Peter *were* in, the family door secured against the legions of burglars and perverts. If he *were* in, he refused, flatly, to go to bed. This meant that lubricity in any form was impossible because he was awake, probably listening, possibly *recording*, and almost certainly drinking the last of the milk and eating the fruit for the children's lunches.

Outsitting him was not feasible strategy. Exhausted by her daily labours at the Ministry of Energy, Mines and Resources and then further exhausted by cooking, homework consultations, and the general wear and tear of motherhood, Martha was red-eyed with fatigue by nine-thirty. Any sexual activity past that hour bordered on necrophilia.

Mornings were an impossible alternative. The differences in their circadian rhythms were such that Martha's eyes sprang open with the dawn chorus while his were blear and his mood surly until eleven-thirty, at which time Martha was beginning to droop.

Weekends were no better and were not exactly weekends. Saturday was his busiest day in the gallery and on Mondays, the traditional closing day for galleries, Martha was, of course, at work in the Ministry of Energy, Mines and Resources. This left Sundays. The logistics of organizing the absence of all three children at the same time and ensuring that absence for at least an hour were next to impossible and if he attempted to hustle her upstairs for a rushed sortie she complained that it didn't seem very 'romantic', a charge that left him stunned.

He had learned not to count his chickens even when Martha and he, by some miracle, lay naked and entwined; open-plan coughing would erupt, open-plan allergies would strike, so that nights which began with tumescent promise ended with the dispensing of Chlor-Triplon and Benedryl.

When she or he returned from these errands of mercy— usually she because of his monstrous and adamantine visibility —she would always say:

I'm sorry, Paul. Do you mind if we don't tonight? It's just that, well, you know ...

He did not, in fact, know *really* what it was that she presumed he knew because *he* would have been capable of enjoying intercourse had the house been under frontal assault by urban guerillas, but he always made polite noises before going into the bathroom and getting his mouth round the gritty-sweet neck of the Benedryl bottle in the hope that the side effects of two disgusting swallows would assist him towards unconsciousness.

Paul had endured these frustrations for years and as far as he could see they could only get worse, because when the other two were a little older they, too, like Peter, would stay up past nine-thirty and would wish to go out and come in.

In his more despondent moments, it seemed likely to Paul that he would not be able to make love to his wife again for ten more years—and that figure was based on the assumption that Jennifer would leave home at eighteen, which was probably being optimistic. At which time, and over his most violent objections, Peter, who would then be twenty-five, and who would have contracted a disastrous marriage, would doubtless be returning to off-load on them damned babies which would be subject every night to croup, grippe, projectile vomiting, and open-plan convulsions.

In ten more years he would be fifty-six.

In ten years after that, if he lived, sixty-six.

He thought about being old; about being him and being old; about being married and being old. He thought of a funny line from a forgotten thriller, an aging lecher who had said that intercourse in the twilight years was all too often like trying to force a piece of Turkish Delight into a piggy bank. Paul was perfectly prepared to accept that this might be so; what depressed him was the almost certain knowledge that he'd still ache to try.

Since his heart attack, or what he persisted in thinking of as his heart attack, he often found himself considering the form and shape of his life. He lived with a great restlessness and longing, as if the frustrations of his semi-celibacy had spread like a malignancy. He did not know what it was he longed for. His life, he felt, was like a man labouring to take a deep breath but being unable to fill out his lungs. Everything, he felt, seemed somehow to be slipping away, fading. He daydreamed constantly, daydreamed of robbing banks, of doing sweaty things with Bianca Jagger, of fighting heroically against BOSS to free Nelson Mandela from Robben Island...Kalashnikov rifles, the pungent reek of cordite...

This restlessness had expressed itself the night before in Montreal in his impulsive purchase at Pinney's Fine Art Auction of a stuffed grizzly bear. Driving back to Ottawa on Highway 17 with the grizzly's torso and snarling head sticking out of the window, he had felt pleased and superior to all the cars which lacked a bear.

Now, he did not wish to think about it.

He lay on his side of the bed listening to the throaty pigeons fluttering and treading behind the fretwork gingerbread which framed the dormer window and rose to one of the twin turrets which were the real reason for his having bought the house.

On the bedside table lay the packet of Nikoban gum.

"Effective as a Smoking Deterrent," he said into the silence of the bedroom, "since 1931."

The other turret rose above the curved end of the bathtub; during the night more granular insulation had sifted down.

He had run out of renovation money eighteen months before. Only the ground floor was finished; the rest of the house looked as if it were in the early stages of demolition. The turret above the bathtub, the renovator had said, could be opened up and finished inside, painted white, lighted possibly, so that when one was lying in the tub it would be rather like looking up the inside of a 'wizard's hat'. Paul remembered his exact words; he remembered the turn of the renovator's wrist and fingers as he conjured this whimsy from the air. All that could be seen through the smashed hole in the ceiling was a dangling sheet of tin or zinc, pieces of two-by-four, and deepening blackness punctured by a point of light. Lying in the tub and gazing up always made Paul think not of the inside of a wizard's hat but of being trapped at the bottom of a caved-in mine shaft.

He bent to examine the wavering arrow. It returned obstinately to 168 lb.; this meant that despite not eating bread at lunch and despite passing up potatoes at dinner he had, in the face of the laws of nature, gained three pounds overnight.

He teased the four white hairs on his chest.

Treat this as a warning, Mr. Denton.

Staring unseeing into the mirror, he pictured himself jogging along the side of the canal, felt the flab over his kidneys jounce. His route unreeled in his mind like the Stations of the Cross: Patterson Avenue, past First, Second, Third, and Fourth Avenues, the stand of pine trees, then the Lansdowne Stadium stretch, and then, rounding the curve, the first sight of the Bank Street bridge. In the final stretch between the Bank Street bridge and the bridge at Bronson, the canal narrowed, the trees overhanging and the bushes crowding in to suggest a sombre tunnel. It was here that he always saw the carp, great silent shapes rising to the scummed surface to suck down floating weed, their lips thick and horny gaping into orange circles.

And then, rubbery legs, breath distressed, almost staggering, into the shadows of the Bronson bridge and out, out to

the canal widening into the blue expanse of Dow's Lake spar-
kling, the open sky, the gentle slopes of the Arboretum on the
far shore, white sails standing on the water.

Treat this as a warning, Mr. Denton.

He had known when the intense pains came that he was
dying and so had done nothing. But Martha had detected it,
something in his face or posture perhaps, and had badgered
him until he'd admitted to some slight discomfort. It was she
who had phoned their doctor and she who had secured him an
emergency appointment. Constriction of the blood vessels
and the muscles of the chest wall caused by tension was
the diagnosis.

Overweight, under-exercised, a pack of cigarettes a day,
tension...*treat this as a warning.*

"You would be wise to avoid," the pompous little fart had
said, "life-situations which generate anxiety and stress."

Paul shook the can of shaving foam, tested the heat of the
water in the basin.

He pulled flesh tight over the angle of his jaw.

How would *you* avoid, he would have liked to ask, how
would *you* avoid being consumed with unsatisfied sexual
desire? *Unsatisfiable* desire, given the combination of Martha's
anxieties and the interior construction of the house. Answer
me that, smug little physician. Go on! What do you suggest?
Castration? Investing in a sound-proofed house? Trading in the
present wife for something a touch more feral? Snuffing the kids?

And *how*, you scrawny little processor of Ontario Health
Insurance Plan cards, how would *you* avoid just the faintest
twinge of anxiety about a business that's barely paying
the rent? A business, furthermore, of which the proprietor
is ashamed.

Two Aspirins and retire to bed?

Keep warm?

And while we're on the subject of tension, stress, anxiety,
surges of adrenalin, and so on and so forth, here's a life-
situation over which you might care to make a couple of magic

passes with your little caduceus. What advice do you have to offer about the best way to avoid one's son?

Yes, son.

S-O-N.

He had noticed the blue-sprayed markings on neighbourhood walls weeks earlier. The script was cramped, busy, fussy squiggles and dots; he had thought it might represent slogans in a foreign language, possibly a very demotic Arabic or Farsi. Given the high concentration of Lebanese in his area, he had thought that these bright blue writings might possibly be charms against the Evil Eye. It had taken weeks of glancing before he'd suddenly recognized them as being in English.

Two of the more decipherable of these mysterious blue messages said:

Check out!

and

(something) *Zod!*

Coming home late one night from a local estate auction at the Ukrainian Hall, which had advertised 'primitive African carvings' that had turned out to be two slick pieces of Makonde junk and a pair of salad servers from Nairobi, he had let himself into the silent house to find in the vestibule a can of blue spraypaint fizzling indelibly onto the newly installed quarry tile.

He had stood there long moments staring.

Paul no longer attempted to deny to himself or to Martha that the presence of his son snagged on his nerves and curdled the food in his stomach. He did not understand the boy; he no longer *wanted* to understand him. It was not unusual for Paul immediately after dinner to be stricken with nervous diarrhea.

Even *thinking* of Peter constricted Paul with rage, made his pulse pound in his neck, throb in the roof of his mouth. He knew that the words 'burst with rage' were no cliché. During these rages, he always found the word 'aneurism' swelling in his mind, pictured a section of artery in his neck or near his heart distending like a red balloon to the very palest of terrifying pinks.

Paul was enraged by his son's appearance, manners, atti-
tudes, reflex hostility, hobbies, and habits. He was reduced to
incoherent anger by the boy's having mutilated all his clothes
by inserting zippers in legs and sleeves, zippers which were
secured by bicycle padlocks, so that he looked like an emaci-
ated scarecrow constructed by a sexual deviant, by his smelly
old draped jackets which he purchased from what he called
'vintage clothes stores', by his bleached hair which he coloured
at weekends with purple food-dye, by his ruminant of a girl-
friend whose mousy hair was bleached in two stripes intersect-
ing at right angles so that she looked like a hot cross bun, by
his wearing loathsome plastic shoes because he didn't want to
be party to the death of an animal, by his advocacy of the
execution of all 'oppressors', which seemed to mean, roughly,
everyone over twenty-five who could read, by his intense
ignorance of everything that had happened prior to 1970, by
his inexplicable and seemingly inexhaustible supply of ready
cash, by his recent espousal of self-righteous vegetarianism,
which was pure and total except for a dispensation in the case
of pepperoni red-hots, by his abandoning in the fridge plastic
containers of degenerating tofu, by his rotten music, by his
membership in an alleged band called The Virgin Exterminators, by his loutish buddies, by the *names* of his loutish
buddies, names which reminded Paul of science fiction about
the primitive descendants of those who'd survived the final
nuclear holocaust, names like Deet, Wiggo, Munchy, *etc.*, by
his diamanté nose-clip and trilby hat, which accessories, in
combination with his dark zippered trousers and draped zippered jacket, gave him the appearance of an Hasidic pervert,
by his endless readiness to chip in with his mindless two bits
concerning: the Baha'i faith, conspiracies, environmental
pollution, the injustice of wealth, fibre-rich food, the compu-
ter revolution, the oppressive nature of parental autho-
rity—*Jesus Christ! Oh, God, was there no end?*—by his festering
bedroom, by his pissing on the toilet seat, by his coming into
his, Paul's, bathroom and removing his, Paul's, box of

Kleenex, by his pallor, his spots, his zits, his dirty long fingernails, his encyclopedic knowledge of carcinogens, his pretentious sipping of Earl Grey tea, his habit of strumming and
chording during dinner on an imaginary guitar, of bursting
into sudden ape-noises, of referring to him, Paul, as 'an older
person', by...*Dear Christ! How he hated that malignant cat with
its obnoxiously pink arsehole!* Misguidedly saved but days ago
from the SPCA without his, Paul's, permission. Not for *his*
bloody son a kitten but a mangy, baleful presence which was
missing one ear and had *things* in the other.

It would, inevitably, shed some of what hair it had left. The
hair would, inevitably, stimulate a new range of allergies in
Jennifer and Alan. The allergy attacks would strike, inevitably, just as the stars stood in rare and fruitful conjunction
leading, inevitably, to yet more nights of throttled rage and
Benedryl.

Paul completed the series of faces indicative of amazed con-
tempt, loathing, rage, and resignation, all of which were
slightly invalidated by the blobs of shaving foam under his ears
and on his Adam's apple, and washed off the razor under the
hot tap. Only a friend, he thought with sudden honesty, could
describe his pectoral muscles as 'muscles'. And even such
minor movement as brushing his teeth set jiggling what once
had been triceps.

Sunlight bathed the hanging plant and lay warm across his
bare feet. His feet were sweaty on the cool tiles. The plant
always received Martha's special attentions. It hung down in
ropes of leaves shaped like miniature bunches of bananas.
Peculiar-looking thing. He chomped with sudden savagery on
the two pieces of Nikoban gum in the hope that this would
release into his bloodstream increased surges of the active
ingredient, lobeline sulphate, effective as a smoking deterrent
since 1931.

He deliberately thought of breakfast as an antidote to
thoughts of a Rothman's King Size. He could have one egg,
medium, boiled, and one slice of toast, dry, with black coffee

for a calorie count of (140) or a small bowl of Shredded Wheat
with no sugar for (150) or a piece of melon, cantaloupe,
medium, one half, for (60). And then, if at lunch he stuffed
his face with alfalfa sprouts or handfuls of grass, he'd be able to
splurge at dinner with a nice bit of tasteless chicken with the
skin removed.

He could feel bad temper tighten and coil.

The bunches-of-bananas plant made him think with exas-
peration and affection of Martha and of the generally peculiar
and incomprehensible nature of life. Martha would soon be
picking off green tomatoes to make chutney, filling the house
with the smell of vats of the evil stuff, onions, vinegar. She did
it every year. No one ever ate the chutney. Not even Martha.
In their various moves, the vintages of preceding years had
accompanied them. The basement was full of the stuff. She put
little labels on the jars. It seemed to be some blind, seasonal
activity like spring-stirred badgers lugging out the old bedding or bower-birds dashing about in the undergrowth collect-
ing shiny stones, though the chutney-making had, so far as he
could see, absolutely no sexual motivation overt or otherwise.
It only made her more tired than usual.

Over the shower rail hung a damp and dwarfish pair of
pantyhose.

The edge of the wash-basin and the counter-top were
freckled, as they were every day, with some dark orange powder she brushed on her face. He wiped it off with a Kleenex as
he did every day. When he put on his bathrobe after his
shower, her plastic shower-cap, always lodged on top of his
bathrobe on the back of the door, would plop onto the floor.

He stood staring at the array of her bottles, unguents and
lotions, creams. With its scarlet cap, there stood the bottle,
the red label: *Dissolvant de polis d'ongles.*

Norma, the girl he'd come to think of as Polly Ongle,
would soon be in the gallery, would soon be busying herself
shining up bits of Ethiopian silver, necklaces, pendants,
Coptic crosses hammered from Maria Theresa *thalers*. He could

picture her working over the glass top of the display case, the curtain of black hair, the incredibly slim waist cinched by the wide, antique Turcoman belt studded with cornelians, her long fingers sorting and stringing old trade beads and copal amber, following the designs in colour photos in *African Arts* magazine.

Since Christmas Eve, he had tried to stop himself thinking about her hands, those slender fingers.

He sighed as he settled himself on the toilet seat.

He enjoyed the emptiness of the house in the mornings, Martha off to work, the deepening silence left behind by the children after the fights about who'd taken this, touched that, *his* lunch had grapes, well *yours* had an orange, the penetrating *shushings* rising to shouts of *Be quiet! Daddy's sleeping!*

This morning hour seemed the only period of complete peace in the entire day.

He reached round behind him for his copy of *The Penguin Book of Modern Quotations*. He placed the box of Kleenex at his feet. Recently, bowel movements had been accompanied by a stream of clear liquid running from his nose. He had thought at first that this was probably the symptom of some terminal disease but as nothing had happened further and he felt relatively healthy he had accepted it as possibly being natural. Though it had never happened to him before and he'd never heard of it happening to anyone else. But, on the other hand, it wasn't the kind of thing likely to crop up in normal conversation.

The bear was worrying him.

He was pleased that he'd had the sense to stow it away in the gallery stockroom before coming home. He could not have stood a morning conversation with Martha about stuffed bears, the questions leading to denunciations and accusations of fecklessness and immaturity, the whole entirely justified harangue shrilling off into the price of sneakers, orthodontistry, day camps, the mounting fines at the Ottawa Public Library because he was so bloody lazy, the price of meat.

"Ha!" he said aloud.

His eye had fallen on an apposite quotation from Frances Cornford concerning Rupert Brooke:

Magnificently unprepared / for the long littleness of life.

He wondered what would have happened to Rupert Brooke if he'd lived long enough to have had a slight paunch, stuff running out of his nose every time he had a crap, and a kid with purple hair. No one was prepared for that. Who could imagine it?

Who in *hell* could he sell a very large bear to?

He wondered what Polly had thought when she'd opened the stockroom and seen six feet three of reared grizzly.

He thought about the Turcoman belt studded with cornelians; he thought about the belt clasping her waist; he tried to stop himself thinking about navels. Shirts or blouses knotted above the waist exposing midriffs, in strong sunshine a down of fine hair glinting...

He had given her the belt for Christmas. He had not told Martha that he had given it to her. He felt vaguely guilty about having given it to her. He felt uncomfortable both about the gift and about keeping it from Martha.

On Christmas Eve, after the flurry of last small sales, he had taken Polly for a Christmas drink. Nothing had happened. They were sitting in a booth at the back of the dimly lit bar. On the wall just above the table was a lamp with a yellowed shade. It cast an almost amber light. She'd been drinking Pernod. She didn't usually speak much; she'd been saying something about the ambassador from Togo who'd been in that morning and who'd been offensively imperious, as he always was.

Her hands were within the pool of amber light. He'd been tranced by the light glinting on the clear nail-polish, hinting as she gestured. That was all. Light, glancing. That was all that had happened.

Paul stiffened and stared at the back of the closed bathroom door.

From below, a doorknob, footsteps.

He gripped the book.

A stream of urine drilling into the toilet bowl.

PETER!

Must have persuaded Martha he was sick.

Probably had an exam.

Or gym.

A loud, moist fart.

Orangutan noises.

> Bam BAM ba-ba Bam
> Bam BAM ba-ba Bam
> Burn DOWN the fuck'n town.

A drawer opening, slamming.

"Dad-ee?"

Creakings up the stairs.

"Oh, Dad-deee!"

Probably peering through the open-plan banisters like something from a zoo.

Only feet away.

Outburst of ape-gibbering.

Pyjama bottoms wrinkled round his ankles, breathing carefully through his open mouth, silently, Paul sat tense on the toilet.

Paul followed what Dr. Leeson called his 'auxiliary' into what Dr. Leeson called, always, 'the inner sanctum'.

"How!" said Dr. Leeson, raising a palm.

Paul smiled.

Dr. Leeson had started greeting Paul in this way some four years earlier after he'd chanced to see in the Ottawa *Citizen* a review of an exhibition of Indian *pechwais* in Paul's gallery. Despite references in the review to India and to Krishna, Ganesh, and Shiva, Dr. Leeson had somehow understood the show to concern Indians from North America. Paul thought the greeting was probably a fair sample of dental humour.

"No more gum trouble? Bleeding?"

Paul shook his head.

"No more looseness in the front here?"

"No, just fine."

"That looseness," said Dr. Leeson, "that can be a sign of adult diabetes but peridontal infection's the—that's it, your head here towards me...*hmm hmmmm—hmm hmmmm...*

Warm peppermint breath.

"*...and broke it apart, Suzanne, Oh my Suzanne!*"

Paul, his eyes pulled open wide, stared over the back of Dr. Leeson's immense hand at the setting sun, an orb in yellow majesty against a wild red deepening to a foreground black. Printed on the blackness of the poster in white were the words:

The goal for my practice is simply to help my patients retain their teeth all of their lives if possible—in maximum comfort, function, health and aesthetics—and to accomplish this appropriately.

Dr. Leeson settled the small rubber nose mask and pulled the tubes high up onto Paul's cheeks. Paul breathed in the thick, slightly sweet gas waiting for the tingling in his hands and feet to start. The mask quickly became slimy, a rubbery smell mixing with the smell of the gas. His mouth was dry. He closed his eyes.

"...up to the lake?" said the auxiliary.

Sounds of instruments on the plastic tray.

"How you doing?"

Paul grunted.

In the coloured darkness, his mind raced. He made a mental note to speak to the kids about picking at the plaster on the second floor. And about not leaving their skateboards in the hall. After this, the bank. Capital Plastics, another phone call that had to be made.

"Relax," said Dr. Leeson, "we're doing good."

As always when the noise started, he felt panicky, felt he must be insane to trust a man younger than himself who wore plaid trousers, felt he *must* check the man's credentials, actually *read* those framed certificates. He felt that no really responsible doctor would wear cowboy boots to work; there was something about the man, something about his large red face and blond eyelashes, which suggested the Ontario Beef Marketing Board; this Leeson, he realized, in whose hands he was, frequented road-houses and rode mechanical bulls.

The steel was in his mouth.

They were talking at a dark remove from him; he had a sudden conviction their relationship was more than dental.

He concentrated on picturing the silent kitchen where for breakfast he'd eaten half a cantaloupe; he conjured up the Boston fern in its earthenware pot, the sleek chrome-and-black-plastic design of the Italian espresso machine Martha had bought him for Christmas, the dark aroma of the coffee beans in the waxed-paper Van Houte bag, cluttering the fridge door the invitations to birthday parties, the shopping lists, medical appointment cards, crayonings of intergalactic battle, all held by Happy Face magnets.

Until he'd heard Peter slamming out of the house, Paul had remained hidden in the bathroom.

On the kitchen counter beside a glass that had contained orange juice, Peter had left a library book. The book was in French. Judging from his report cards and the comments of Mrs. Addison on the last Parent-Teachers Evening, he'd be entirely incapable of reading it. The book was entitled *C'est Bon La Sexualité* and contained diagrams of wombs.

Sitting there in the whiteness of the kitchen, the sunshine, the silence, Paul had been moved by a surge of pity and compassion.

He was swallowing water; could feel wetness on his cheek.

He tried to think, deliberately, of what was to be done that day.

Letters to go out, bulk mailing, for the exhibition of Shona stone carving. The photo-copy place. Capital Plastics to price lucite bases for the Mossi flutes. Rosenfeld in Washington to deal with over the crate of pre-Columbian pots; Customs. A new rubber ring-thing—what *was* the word?—rubber *belt* for the carpet part of the vacuum-cleaner.

The carpet in the gallery was coir matting, suitably simple and primitive, hard on the vacuum-cleaner's wheels and brushes.

The word 'coir' made him think of 'copra', 'coitus', 'copulation'.

Nearly everything did.

The current exhibition at the Uhuru Gallery of Primitive Arts was a collection, on consignment, of modern Makonde carvings, every single one of which he loathed. Preceding them had been exhibitions of contemporary 'temple' carvings from India, shadow-puppets from Indonesia, *papier-mâché* anthropomorphic frogs from Surinam, garish clay airplanes from Mexico, and drawings from the remote highlands of New Guinea executed in Magic Marker.

Soon it would be twenty years since his life had taken the turn which had led him to where he was now. Okoro Training College. Port Harcourt. Sometimes when he looked through the old snapshots in the chocolate box he felt he was looking at preposterous strangers: Martha with long black hair tied back with a ribbon; he wearing ridiculous British khaki shorts and knee socks; Martha standing with Joseph, the houseboy, in his shabby gown, long splayed toes; Mr. Oko Enwo in his academic gown; he and Joseph posing on either side of a dead snake slung over the compound clothesline.

Strangers.

Sun-bleached strangers.

At first, the gallery had done well; he had sold, cheaply, many of the good carvings he'd collected in Nigeria. But then what small supply there was dried up. The young men were drifting from the ceremonies of the dance to the beer-hall bands and city discos. The world he'd been privileged to glimpse on holiday expeditions to those Igbo villages upcountry all those years ago had been even then a world close to extinction, a world about to be swept away on a tide of plastic sandals, cheap stainless steel watches from Russia, Polaroid cameras, calculators.

The Uhuru Gallery, which had opened with passion and vision, had become little more than an emporium of Third World tourist junk. The only genuine carving on his walls was a stern Bambara mask whose austerity was a daily rebuke.

He dreamed sometimes still of the journeys upcountry jammed in the back of the rackety Bedford lorries which served as buses, journeys of dust and shimmering heat which ended in the packed excitement of the village commons surrounded by the mud walls and thatch of the compounds.

Often he had been offered a seat of honour among the elders in the shade, while Martha had been packed in with the women and the glistening children, the sun splintering through the leaves and fronds of the trees beyond the compounds.

And then the tranced hours of the festival, glasses of palm wine cloudy green, the sun beating down and the air pulsing with the rhythms of the four drummers, quivering with the notes of the gongs and the village xylophone, shush-shuffle of seed-rattles. Muzzle-loaders exploding into the blue signalled the approach of the procession from the Men's House of the cloth and raffia-clad masks—*beke, igri, mma ji, mkpe, umurumu*—individual dancers breaking from the chorus to raise the red dust until their feet were lost in the haze.

Then the slow unfolding of the story-songs, the high call and response of the two leaders, the great wave of sound from behind the painted masks. And between the stories, the masked dancers burrowing into the crowd to demand 'dashes', the lines of *akparakpa* dancers in parody of female dancing, each man wearing thick rolls of women's plastic waist beads, buttocks stuck out, greeted by the women with shrieks of *aiy aiy aiy aiy aiy.* Until there seemed no end, the drums sounding inside one's head, the notes of the xylophone vibrating, gong and slit-drum, dust, sun, the praise-sayers, the singing.

"Mr. Denton?"

"Umm?"

The chair rising to an upright position.

"Mr. Denton! You're all finished now. I'm going to leave you just on the oxygen for a couple of minutes, okay? Like we usually do? Okay?"

He opened his eyes.

Yellow. Red. Black patterned with white marks.

"Fine. Sorry. Yes, sure."

He lay staring at the poster of the setting sun against the wild red sky.

The fragrance from a tangle of wild roses in front of a house on Gilmour Street lay heavily on the humid air. Paul stopped to breathe it in; it was almost indecent. His teeth felt foreign. Exploring them with his tongue, he turned onto Elgin Street. After the darkness of the gas, after the strange shapes of chairs, carpets, counters, the buttons in the elevator, had once again assumed their form and function and steadied into place, he always felt almost resurrected when he walked out into the world.

Sunlight glittering on spokes and rims. Back straight, fingertips of one hand on top of the handlebars, a girl on a ten-speed bike coasting in towards the red light. White top, blue linen skirt, she jutted like a ship's figurehead. Just before she drew level, she swooped to apply her brakes. Staring into an abyss of pristine cleavage, Paul stumbled over an Airedale terrier and babbling apologies shot through the doorway into Mike's Milk.

After prolonged dental torture, nerves stretched to breaking-point, *one* cigarette, he reasoned, was understandable and forgivable; he was not really letting himself down; he would probably throw away the rest of the package. Or perhaps ration them judiciously, using them in conjunction with the Nikoban gum to effect a more *rational* withdrawal; it was, he thought, an unrealistic and possibly injurious strain on the system to diet, jog, and stop smoking all at the same time.

With some five minutes in hand before the bank opened, he strolled down Elgin Street. The cigarette tasted so wonderful that he felt he ought to be smoking it through a long onyx holder. His trousers seemed definitely looser at the waist. He crossed against red lights.

Standing in the line-up idly watching the top halves of tellers, he thought about the girl with the huge hoop earrings, wisps of hair escaping from her collapsing bun, the absent eyes. Unless she was in the vault, she wasn't on duty. Oddly *Victorian*-looking girl. As one might imagine the daughter of an impoverished rural vicar in an old novel. He suspected she was profoundly crazy and was attracted by the idea of whatever mayhem or enforced redistribution of wealth she might be capable of. Once when he hadn't seen her in the bank for some weeks, he'd asked her if she'd been sick.

Oh, no, she'd said, *I'm a floater.*

He still wondered what she'd meant and why he kept on thinking about it.

Despite the air-conditioning, the cheques were wilting in his hand. Beside him, a rack containing deposit slips, brochures about Registered Retirement Savings Plans, copies of that month's Royal Bank Letter entitled: *Regarder la mort en face.* The next shuffle forward brought him round the curve of the furry blue rope and closer to the counter; he stood watching the outline of panties beneath the slacks of the teller who was waiting at the central cage for cash.

He walked on up Elgin past the National Gallery and the National Arts Centre. Before crossing towards the Château Laurier, he paused to glance in the window of the Snow Goose at the latest display of native Canadian arts, alleged Haida masks, horrible great green lumps of Eskimo soapstone. Not, he thought, with sudden heaviness of spirit, that he could afford to feel superior; they were no worse than Indonesian frogs with hats on. He decided to phone the Snow Goose later to see if they'd like a nice grizzly bear; just the thing to pull in tourists and their kids. Stick it out on the sidewalk opposite the London double-decker tour bus.

He had promised Jennifer and Alan to bring home those plastic things from the bank for saving a dollar's worth of pennies and had forgotten; he had promised Jennifer bubble-gum with Star Wars cards inside. If he could have raised ten thousand dollars, he'd have bid the night before in Montreal on all the Sepik River lots, bid against Mendelson, and against Lang, Klein, too. What a delight it would have been to have mounted a genuine exhibition, authentic tribal art, masks and boards made long before the luxury boats started pulling into the river bank villages to disgorge the corruption of tourists. But the whole game was climbing beyond his reach. He thought of the dinner he'd had on rue St. Denis before the auction, a street completely changed since his day. And walking along Sussex Drive towards the Uhuru, he found himself thinking for some reason or other of a rented room in a house on rue Jeanne Mance.

Strange that after all those years he could still see the room so clearly after he'd been in it only once; strange, too, that he had only the vaguest memory of the girl. He could see the frayed central hole in the threadbare carpet, the paperbacks on the mantelpiece between two white-painted bricks, empty Chianti bottles strung above, the mobile, tarot cards, Braque poster of white dove, vast glass carboy containing moulting bulrushes, the brass incense-burner in the shape of a Chinese lion...

He remembered how intensely excited he'd been returning with her to her room after an afternoon drinking Québerac — *that* was what he remembered so clearly. The intensity of it. It wasn't simply sexual anticipation but something more complicated, more difficult to think about, mysterious. A room— bed, hotplate, wash-basin—was so much more private than a house. Being in a stranger's room, a room that contained the bed in which she slept, a room which was furnished with the things that were hers, entering into that privacy was somehow at that moment more intimate, more exciting than nakedness.

There had been a pink facecloth, he remembered, draped over the edge of the basin.

It was the revealing, the unfolding, the unfurling, the opening up of what had been closed that excited him, the sense that this intimacy—difficult to put this into words, difficult to think of the feeling—the sense that this intimacy could draw him into a new...well, *current* suggested the sort of thing, a current that would carry him out from the mundane shores, sweep him into the violent invigoration of white water.

So far as he could remember, the intimacy had dissipated in suddenly awkward talk. Of what, he wondered?

Some comically pretentious nonsense.

The wisdom of the Upanishads, perhaps.

In those now distant undergraduate days at Sir George Williams University, he'd spent much of his time with the arty crowd in the various cafés on Stanley Street, the Riviera, Carmen's, The Pam-Pam, The Seven Steps, Marvin's Kitchen. Sitting for hours over a single cup of coffee, he'd yearned after the arty girls, the girls who sat with guys who'd published poems. Arty girls then had all looked much the same. Hair very long and straight with bangs, faces mask-like with make-up, eyes rimmed with black. Black turtlenecks, black skirts, black mesh stockings. The way they all looked, it all had something to do with Paris, Sartre, existentialism, and a movie starring Juliette Greco. He wondered if Sartre was still alive and hoped not.

And the artiest ones of all, he remembered, wore green nail polish and white lipstick. How had he forgotten that? That lipstick. And ballet slippers. And handmade silver earrings. And carried huge handmade leather bags. And they'd all looked anorectic and temptingly *unwholesome*, as though they'd lend themselves, impassively, to amazing sexual practices. Not that Polly Ongle was at all like those girls. But there was something of all that about her. Something of that sort of stance. She was, he suspected the same *sort* of girl.

"*Tabarouette!*" said the waitress, depositing on their table a bowl of potato chips. "Me, I'm scared of lightning!"

Turning the glass vase-thing upside down, she lighted the candle inside.

"Cider?" she repeated.

"No?" said Paul.

"Oh, well," said Norma, "I'll have what-do-you-call-it that goes cloudy."

"Pernod," said Paul. "And a Scotch, please."

"Ice?"

"They feel squishy," said Norma, stretching out her leg.

"Umm?"

"My sandals."

He looked down at her foot.

It was the Happy Hour in the bar on the main floor of the Château Laurier. People drifting in were pantomiming distress and amazement as they eased out of sodden raincoats or used the edge of their hands to wipe rain from eyebrows and foreheads. Men were seating themselves gingerly and loosening from their knees the cling of damp cloth; women were being casually dangerous with umbrellas. Necks were being mopped with handkerchiefs; spectacles were being polished with bar napkins.

"Well," said Paul, raising his glass, "home and dry. Cheers! Thank God for that old umbrella of yours."

She smiled and made a small gesture with her glass.

"What's this obsession you seem to have with cider?" said Paul.

"It's not an obsession. It's just that it doesn't have chemicals in it, that's all. It's just straight juice."

"Well, not *quite* straight," said Paul.

She shrugged.

"But I don't use alcohol much at all usually."

"Not like this stuff," said Paul, tapping his glass. "It's supposed to be full of some sort of stuff—estrogen?—no, a word something like that. *Esters*, is it? Some sort of *oils*. Begins with 'e', I think. Anyway, supposed to be *very* bad for you."

"You shouldn't do things that are bad for you."

"Well, that sounds a bit boring," said Paul, smiling. "Now and again, things that are bad for you are fun."

Norma stirred her ice-cubes with the plastic paddle.

"No?" said Paul.

"Maybe," she said.

Small talk, chat, flirtation, all were uphill work with Polly. Silence didn't seem to bother her one bit. She was usually rather taciturn and—not grumpy exactly—but perhaps 'contained' was the word. Or 'detached'. She gave the impression of being always an observer. She reminded him uncomfortably at times of Jennifer. Once when Jennifer had been four or five, he'd taken her to a zoo where she'd considered the llama over which he was enthusing and had said,

'What's it for?'

He was painfully aware that he seemed unable to strike the right tone, that his chatter sounded less flirtatious than avuncular. The whole situation made him feel like an actor in a hopeless play, plot implausible, dialogue stilted.

He glanced again at the dangling sandal. They were rather elegant. They were what he thought were called buffalo-thongs, just a sort of leather ring which held the sandal on the foot by fitting round the big toe. Her toes were long and distinctly spaced, not cramped together, the little toes not at all deformed by shoes. He wondered how that was possible. They were almost like fingers. He felt an urge to trace their length with his fingertip.

"Pardon?"

"I said, 'Do you know where the washroom is?'"

He watched her threading her way through the tables. The black harem pants were loose and baggy but in places, as she moved, very much *not* loose and baggy. All through the hot, close afternoon he'd been disturbingly aware of them. Her slimness, the tautness of her body, her carriage, she moved like a dancer; the silk scarf knotted round her waist as a belt added to the suggestion. In the patches of spotlighting, the white cotton top glowed blue and purple.

It was irritating him that he couldn't remember the name of the carcinogens that, according to Peter, Scotch was supposed to contain. He had, God knew, heard it often enough. And Polly's saying that she didn't 'use alcohol much' also reminded him of Peter; it was an expression always used by Peter in some such formula as, 'Older people use alcohol but young people prefer soft drugs'; the expression irritated him on a variety of fronts.

At the next table, the two ghastly government women were still trading acronyms. The older, dykey woman's voice was husky. In front of her was a large round tin of tobacco and a packet of Zigzag cigarette papers. Her lipstick was thickly applied and shiny; when her face was in the light from the candle, he could see a faint smear of lipstick on her front teeth. Her bechained spectacles hung down the front of her beige linen suit. She kept relighting the cigarettes with a flaring Zippo lighter. As she talked, she was scattering ashes. Paul thought that in some way he didn't understand she was being cruel; there was something in the conversation of cat and mouse. The younger, softer-looking woman had fluffy hair and was wearing a blazer; the brass buttons glinted.

Oh, I do so agree! said the older, rapacious one. *David's a heaven guy. Just a heaven guy! But there's the problem of Beth, baby girl.*

But Beth's just not a mainstream person.

Well, yes, darling, agreed—and therewith you win the coconut.

Paul signalled to the waitress for another round.

What Beth needs, baby girl, is a vote of confidence from life.

But I thought there was consensus...

Darling, said the other, sticking out the tip of her tongue and picking off a shred of tobacco and then leaning forward and placing her hands over the younger woman's hand, *let's approach what one might call the nub.*

He saw Polly coming back through the tables and stood up.

"Look, I'll just be a minute," he said. "Got to go myself."

Once out of the bar, he wandered into the hotel lobby in search of a public phone. He was directed past a florist's and a showcase exhibiting portraits by Karsh. He found that he'd travelled more or less in a circle and had ended up at the rear entrance to the bar. The phones were between the two washrooms. As he was looking for a quarter, a woman in an elaborate bridal outfit came out of the washroom. Two other brides followed her. Pinned on the bosoms of the brides were buttons the size of saucers which said: Happy Occasions Inc.

"Honey?" an American man was saying. "Yeah. I'm in Ottawa. It's the capital of Canada. We're coming into Kennedy tomorrow in the morning."

Paul listened to the ringing.

"Martha? Everything okay?"

"I'm in the Château Laurier having a drink."

"No, just a bit damp. I managed to get in here before it really got started. And you? Did you get a cab?"

"What? Can't hear you. It's all crackly and your voice keeps fading."

"Well, that's what I'm phoning for. I'm not sure exactly when. I've arranged to meet a guy here to look at some photographs of carvings he wants to sell. If he ever shows up in all this. So I don't really know."

"No, no. You go ahead. Eat with the kids and if I get back I'll get a sandwich or something. And if I'm going to be late, I'll probably get something out somewhere. Okay? So don't worry about it."

"No. There's no reason why I should be. But if I am, don't wait up for me. But I won't be."

"Don't forget tomorrow's *what?*"

"*Garbage* day! Thought you said 'Harbour'. Yes, I'll put it out when I get back."

"The meat tray in the fridge—I got that bit."

"Salami. Good."

"What do you mean?"

"How *can* I be careful? Please, for God's sake, don't start one of these. If lightning is going to strike me, Martha, what can I do to prevent it?"

"Yes, okay. I promise not to go near metal street-lights."

"No. I'm not just saying it."

"Love you, too. 'Bye."

"What?"

"Alan lost his *what*?"

"I'll speak to him tomorrow."

"'Bye."

"Yes."

"'Bye."

He wandered back into the hotel lobby and pushed out through the revolving doors. The wind was chilly. He stood under the noisy canvas awning. The rain was still lashing down with a violence that reminded him of the rains in Africa; it was as if the asphalt of Wellington Street had quickened into a broad river. He stood watching the rain pock the surface of the sheets and rills of water flooding down towards Rideau Street.

Just off the main lobby near the entrance to the bar were the windows of an art gallery. He stood there. It had recently changed hands. The stock, however, looked much the same. He stood staring at all the landscapes, the still-lifes, the flowers in vases, the paintings of decrepit barns and split-rail fences, the paintings involving horses, maple syrup, logs.

He could have told her he was sitting out the storm with Norma without bothering her in the slightest. There was no reason not to have told her. Amazingly, she seemed to think of Norma as a pleasant enough girl who was useful in the gallery; she'd once said that Norma would look so much more present-able if only she'd do something about her hair.

He stared at a large, gilt-framed picture which was exhibited on an easel; lumpy purple mountains, the central lake, the maple trees. It could as easily have been the other view: lumpy mountains, central lake, foreground rock, jack pines. It was all the same, the same sort of thing as Eskimo carvings and frogs from Surinam with hats on.

After the Makonde, the Shona stone.

As he walked through the archway and into the bar, he saw that the two government women had left, and felt an odd sense of relief.

"It's still absolutely pouring out there," he said, sitting down and hitching the chair closer. "And the sky's still black with it. Hasn't that waitress come yet?"

"Paul?"

"What?"

"You know, Paul," she said, leaning forward to rest her arms on the table, "I've been thinking."

"What about?"

"You really *ought* to take better care of yourself."

"Pardon?"

"Well, you can't just ignore it."

"Ignore what?"

"The trouble you had with your ... your chest. Those pains."

"You're losing me. How did we get onto *this*?"

"What we were saying before. About cider. About drinking things that can damage your body."

"Oh! I see. Well, what are you trying to suggest? That I drink too much?"

"No, of course not. But..."

"Sound," said Paul, opening his jacket and tapping himself over the heart, "as a bell. Lively as a two-year-old. Chirpy as a cricket. Fit as the proverbial fiddle."

"Don't *joke* about it!"

He stared at her across the table, at her eyes, the long eyelashes somehow accentuated by the glow from the candle below. The candlelight was picking up auburn tints in the sweep of her black hair.

"What's all this great seriousness in aid of, Norma?"

"You don't have to treat me as if I'm a child!"

"I wasn't aware that I was. I don't. But what I mean is, what brought all this on? I mean, so suddenly?"

"No reason."

"Well, what are you so annoyed about?"

She shrugged.

"Norma?"

She concentrated on stirring about the remains of her ice cubes.

"Hello?"

"It shouldn't take a genius," she said, "to work it out."

The waitress placed the Pernod and the Scotch on the brown napkins, glanced through the checks on her tray, propped their check between the bowl of chips and a triangular cardboard sign advertising a specialty of the house, a drink involving rye whisky, Piña Colada Mix, orange juice, egg whites, and a maraschino cherry.

It was called Sunset Flamenco.

He couldn't think of anything to say.

Norma was sitting back in her chair, head bent, plying the plastic paddle. He stared at the white line of the part in her hair.

He felt—he wasn't sure *what* he felt. It was many, many years since he'd played verbal footsie with girls in bars. If she'd meant what he *thought* she'd meant, the situation seemed to be opening up to possibilities he'd tried to stop himself thinking about for months. But it was entirely possible that she hadn't meant to imply what he thought she'd meant to imply, that the inferences he'd drawn were influenced by desire, by watching all afternoon the folds and furrows of the matte black material of those harem pants...but it certainly *felt* as if the inference he'd drawn was what had been intended.

He drained his glass of Scotch.

"Ah . . . ," he said, "you know what I think would be a good idea? If it's all right with you, I mean. If you haven't got anything planned. Norma?"

"What?"

"Well, as it's still pouring, if we had dinner here together. What do you think?"

"No, I haven't got anything planned."

"So would you like to?"

"Why not?" she said. "Sure."

"Good!" he said. "I'd like that."

He glanced at his watch.

"It's a bit early yet," he said, "so if you think our bodies could stand the strain, we'll sit for a bit over another drink. Okay?"

She nodded.

He wished he hadn't used the word 'bodies'.

He lighted a cigarette.

"I thought you'd quit," she said.

He blew out a long, deep jet of smoke.

"I am in the process of quitting."

"Is it—" she said.

"I think—" he said. "Sorry. What were you ..."

"No," she said.

"I was just going to say that I think there's supposed to be a band."

"Where?"

"In the restaurant."

"What sort of band?"

"I don't know. A dance band, I suppose. It's supposed to be quite good. The restaurant, I mean."

"Do you like dancing?" she said.

"Not much, I'm afraid. Do you?"

"It depends."

"You *look* like a dancer."

"What do you mean?"

"A professional dancer."

She smiled.

"What's funny?"

"I was thinking about you dancing."

"So what's funny about that?"

"I couldn't imagine it."

"Why not?"

She shrugged.

"Well, in the gallery you always seem so...oh, I don't know."

"Seem so what?"

"Well...*dignified.*"

"What do you mean, exactly, by 'dignified'?"

"I mean...I couldn't imagine you dancing."

"Let me tell you," he said, "that in the days of my youth..."

"You're not old," she said.

"Well, of course I'm not *old* but..."

"You're *not*," she said. "You shouldn't say that."

She was staring at him with uncomfortable intensity.

He decided it would be a very good idea to go to the washroom again.

It was empty and echoey in the washroom and smelled of the cakes of cloying air-freshener stuff in the urinals, a smell that he was rather ashamed of not disliking. He examined himself in the mirrors and combed his hair. All he'd had for lunch had been a container of yoghurt. He was beginning to feel the effects of the Scotch.

He thought of Polly's eyelashes.

Like Bambi.

What else *could* she have meant?

To the blank tile wall facing him, he said in a deliberately boomy voice,

"Bum like a plum."

In the farthest cubicle, someone stirred, shoes grating on tiled floor.

Paul coughed.

Facing them just inside the entrance of the Canadian Grill as they waited for the *maître d'* stood a sort of Islamic tent.

It was octagonal. It was large enough to have slept two. But higher. It rose to an ornate finial. Or rather, it was *tent-like.*

Gauzy, chiffony stuff was stretched over the eight ribs. The shape suggested something of the dome of a mosque or a Mogul helmet. On a platform inside stood a huge basket of artificial flowers.

Paul stared at this amazing thing wondering who could have imagined such a folly in a Canadian National Railways Hotel in a room whose decor seemed otherwise baronial.

Or it might have been intended to suggest a miniature band-stand.

Or a gazebo.

"I don't think I'm dressed for this," whispered Norma.

"Nonsense," he said. "You look beautiful."

He smiled at her.

"As a matter of fact," he said, "you *always* look beautiful."

He followed her down the acres of tartan carpet, the khaki army-surplus bag bumping on her hip. Sticking out of it towards him was the shiny black handle of a hairbrush. The *maître d'* was a short, gorilla-shaped man in a bulging tuxedo. He kept hitching at his white gloves. His face was battered and as he walked he moved his head and shoulders as if shadow-boxing.

At a table at the edge of the dance floor, the *maître d'* heaved out Norma's chair with his left hand and, raising his right, with his gloved fingers fumbled a silent snap. They sat and were overwhelmed by waiters. Waiters seemed to outnumber customers. The waiters wore tuxedos but the servers and their servitors wore brown outfits with orange lapels; the width of the lapels seemed to indicate gradations of rank. Narrow lapels poured glasses of water. Wide lapels placed baskets of bread. Tuxedos inquired if they desired an apéritif.

"Scotch," said Paul.

"What a weird man!" said Norma.

"Which?"

"That head waiter."

"He's a retired boxer," said Paul.

"How do you know?"

"Undefeated CN/CP Bantam Champion."

"Really?"

"They use him for thumping temperamental chefs."

"Oh, he isn't!"

"Customer complaints a specialty."

"I've never been in a place like this," said Norma.

It was as if the decorator had attempted to marry vague notions of a baronial Great Hall with the effects of an old movie theatre. Diners formed islands in the room's vast emptiness.

"Wine?" said Paul to the waiter. "Oh, I would think so but we haven't decided yet what we want to eat."

They opened the padded leatherette menus.

"*L'omble de l'Arctique*," said Paul.

"Oh, look!" said Norma. "Behind you, look!"

"What *is* an Arctic omble?"

"Paul, look!"

Waiters were converging.

A party of nine all of whom seemed to have ordered roast beef.

Narrow lapels were hurrying in bearing aloft silver-coloured covered dishes; servers were pushing up to the table wheeled heating grills; servitors were lighting the gas. Wide lapels were taking the dishes from the narrow lapels and were handing them to the tuxedos, who plucked off the domed lids and slid the dishes onto the flames, poking artistically at the contents with spoon and fork until the gravy was boiling briskly.

An atmosphere of muted hysteria gripped the drama. There was much tense French-Canadian cursing. Chafing-dish lids were left with an edge in the flames so that narrow lapels burned their fingers removing them; a Yorkshire pudding fell on the floor; lapel bumped into lapel; dishes forgotten on the flames sent up fatty smoke as the gravy burned onto them.

"Tell him!" said Norma.

"Monsieur?"

"Your napkin thing," said Paul, pointing. "On your arm. Appears to be on fire."

Norma was hidden behind her menu giggling.

"Value for money, eh?" he said.

He was beginning to feel merrily sloshed.

The smouldering napkin was rushed from the room in a covered dish.

The acrid smell lingered.

One of the waiters was touring the table with a gravy boat; his progress was sacerdotal. Each time he stooped to dispense horseradish, his abbreviated jacket rose, revealing under his rucked shirt the elasticized top of his underwear.

"You know what it's all like?" said Paul. "It's like a Fernandel movie or Jacques Tati. That film he made about a restaurant. What *was* that called? The one that came before *Traffic?*"

"Are they French?"

"The reason *is*," said Paul, "the reason it's all a bit off-centre, is because it's a railway hotel. All these Bowery Boys aren't *real* waiters. They're all guys off *trains*—the guys that put the hot-dogs in the microwave ovens at the take-out counter place. The guys that are grumpy about serving you once you've passed Kingston because it takes them two hundred miles with their lips moving to fill in the sheets about how many sandwiches they've sold. Which are full of ice crystals anyway. And after years of loyal service on the Montreal-Toronto run, they're all rewarded with a job here on land. Which is why there's so many of them. And look! Here he is. He's coming again."

They watched the bobbing and weaving of the *maître d'* as he led a couple to a nearby table.

"The Caboose Kid," said Paul.

"What?"

"That's the name he used to fight under. No. That's not quite right, is it? *Kid Caboose!* That's it. That's better."

"Honestly!" said Norma. "You're so *silly.*"

Head on one side, she was considering him.

"You really get into it, don't you?"

"What do I 'get into'?"

"All this stuff you make up."

He shrugged and smiled at her.

"Do I?"

He was beginning to find it difficult to keep his mind on what his lips were saying. For some moments, he'd been aware of her leg touching his beneath the table; this contact was generating a most marvellous warmth. The play of the matte black material filled his mind, furling, fitting plump, furrowed. Through his lower body and down his thighs seeped a different kind of warmth, luxurious, languorous, as if he were bleeding heavily from the hot centre of a painless wound.

He knew that he ought to be saying something.

He glanced across at her.

"Oh! Are those new?"

"What?"

"Those earrings. Hadn't noticed them."

With the back of her hand, she lifted and steered away the weight of her hair. This movement and the cocking of her head tensed the tendon down the side of her neck and raised her left breast towards him.

What he had intended as an *mmmm!* of appreciation broke from him as something closer to a groan.

"It's lovely," he said.

"Vous avez choisi?"

Startled, Paul glanced up.

"Pardon? Oh, I don't know. Ah, Norma?"

"Oh," she said, and opened the menu again.

"Oh, I don't know. I'd like a steak, I think."

"L'entrecôte, madame?"

"I guess so."

"Monsieur?"

"*L'omble de l'Arctique à l'infusion d'anis,*" said Paul. "What *is* it?"

"L'omble de l'Arctique," said the waiter, "it is a fish."

"What kind of fish?"

"That's a pink fish."

"Pink," repeated Paul.

"Inside the fish," said the waiter, gesturing with pad and ballpoint, "is pink."

An arm removed the ashtray and replaced it with a clean one; cutlery was set; the *sommelier* performed upon foil and cork. Paul duly tasted the grotesquely overpriced Mouton Cadet, remembering when it had been available for the present price of a pack of cigarettes and not much of a bargain even then.

She raised her glass and touched it to his.

Bambi.

Light danced off the polished tops of the salt and pepper shakers, flashed off cutlery. He watched the wink of light inside his glass, the play of pinks cast on the tablecloth. He was aware of light and shadow above him. He was, he realized, more inebriated than he'd thought. He tried the word 'inebriated' inside his head. It seemed to work perfectly.

The brown sleeve placed under him a shrimp cocktail.

He stared down into it.

"Et pour madame, les hors d'oeuvres variés."

The shrimps were minuscule, greyish and frayed. He speared one. It was limp and didn't taste of anything at all. He would have sworn under oath that the sauce was a combination of ketchup and Miracle Whip.

"It's not good?" said Norma.

"Try it," said Paul. "Here. I'll put some on your plate."

"No," she said. "Just give me some on your fork."

Holding the fork poised, she said,

"Paul?"

"What?"

"You didn't really think I'd mind, did you?"

"Mind what?"

"Using your fork," she said. "I don't."

He watched her lips close over the tines.

From behind the stage curtains with their flounced valance, a tuning 'A' sounded three times on a piano. It was approximated by a guitar.

She wrinkled her nose.

"It's not special, is it?" she said, handing back the fork.

Three ascending trumpet notes sounded.

The last one cracked.

The curtains drew back to reveal the resident band. They all wore baby-blue blazers and blue shirts with blue ruffles. They looked dispirited. The trumpet player spoke too close to the microphone so that the only words Paul caught were what sounded like 'block and tackle' and 'for your dining pleasure' and then they launched into "The Tennessee Waltz".

After they'd worked it through, there was scattered applause.

"Oh, groan," said Norma. "Groan. Groan."

"This place," said Paul, "is beginning to make me feel about ready for my pension."

"You know what we ought to do?"

"What?"

"Well, if you feel like it, I mean."

"Like what?"

She paused.

"I think," she said, "that you're beginning to get spliffed."

"Spliffed? Oh! Certainly not," he said. "Here, in an amazing exhibition of total clarity, is precisely what you said. You said that you'd like to do something if I felt like it but you didn't say what. You see?"

"Go somewhere where there's some non-plastic music."

"Where's that?"

"I know somewhere. Would you like to?"

"A magical mystery tour?"

Accented with rattles, wood-blocks, and a cow-bell, the band started hacking at something vaguely Latin-American.

"Well," said Paul, "nothing could be much worse than this."

"Oh, look!" she said. "I think this is us."

A wheeled grill was advancing on their table; domed dishes held on high were heading in their direction; servitors were congregating.

The mummery commenced.

When bits of this and clumps of that had been arranged and rearranged, the plates were set before them.

"Eh, voilà!" said the waiter.

Beside the chunk of fish was a plump greyish thing whose outer layers were almost translucent; these translucent leaves were heavily veined; they looked like veined membranes, like folded wings; whatever it was resembled the cooked torso of a giant insect.

They studied it.

"Could it be one of those things you get in salads?"

"Oh!" said Paul. "An endive? I suppose it *could* be. Braised?"

It reminded him of the nightmare things he'd batted down with a tennis racquet in their bedroom in Port Harcourt. He pressed it with his fork and yellow liquid issued.

He pushed the plate away.

He summoned a waiter.

He studied the brandy's oily curve on the side of the glass. Changing with the angle of the glass, the brandy's colours reminded him of stain and varnish, of the small chest of drawers he'd promised to strip and refinish. He tipped and tilted the glass; oak, amber, the colours in the centre exactly the colours of the patina on rubbed and handled carvings.

After the Makonde carvings, the Shona stone.

And after the Shona stone, Rosenfeld's pre-Columbian pots, and after Rosenfeld's pots...he looked down a dreary vista of crafts elevated to the status of art wondering if the honest thing wouldn't be a return to teaching.

He thought of the years after his return from Nigeria, years no longer cushioned by a salary from CIDA and a government house, the years he'd spent languishing at Lisgar Collegiate. What with the compelling arguments of Martha, the baby, the mortgage payments, he'd tried to persuade himself that he cared about teaching and the minutiae of school life, but the future had yawned before him, mountains of exercise-books in which until the age of sixty-five he'd be distinguishing with a red pencil between 'their' and 'there'.

Uhuru!

He grunted.

And after Rosenfeld's pots...

He was startled by the applause.

A girl had come out onto the stage. She was blonde and pretty. She was wearing a long green dress, the sort of dress that Paul thought of as a 'party dress'. Her voice was small but sweet.

He found that he was humming along audibly with the melody of "These Foolish Things". And then began to find his phrasing diverging from hers. He was so used to Ella Fitzgerald's version of the song that he was anticipating adornment and shading which this girl could never reach. Pretty but somehow asexual, she was a crunchy-granola girl, an advertisement girl, impossibly wholesome, a toothpaste girl, under her party dress and white immaculate undies as waxen and undifferentiated as a doll.

He breathed in the brandy's rising bouquet. Opening the pack of Rothman's King Size, his fingers fumbled to discover that there were only two left. He somehow had smoked twenty-three cigarettes since ten o'clock in the morning.

The girl was singing "Ev'ry Time We Say Goodbye".

When, he wondered, could he have smoked them?

Tried to recall; tried to count.

He was moved and moving with the melody, could feel his head swaying.

He closed his eyes.

> *...how strange the change*
> *from major to minor*
> *ev'ry time we say goodbye.*

Behind the girl's voice, he seemed to hear Ella's voice, dark and brooding.

He'd always liked the song, thought it the best of Cole Porter's, the least offensively clever, one of the few where intelligence and emotion seemed to marry.

He gazed into the snifter, amber light fragmenting, sipped. The song was drawing to its close.

...from major to minor
ev'ry time we say goodbye.

He thought about that. Admired the subtlety, the poetry, admired the line's *movement*. Was 'elegance' the word he was looking for? Partly. It was partly that. But it was also *true*. Things *did* move from major to minor. Though in *his* case it was more minor to major, more a question of hello—the long day in the Uhuru and then the anticipation on the homeward journey, *the seeing her*. But major to minor, minor to major— that didn't, so far as he could see, change the *point*. Change the point of what the song *said*.

He suddenly found himself groping.

What?

Said?

Said what?

He considered the possibility of his being drunk. His thoughts seemed to be moving slowly, thickly, as if viscous, somehow like the brandy in the glass. Which added up to roughly (200) calories. He patted his pockets, listening for the rattle of the Nikoban gum. He attempted the painful mental arithmetic of computing the number of calories he'd drunk; it was hard; large numbers were involved; it seemed to total somewhere in the region of (2,000).

Not taking into account two bowls of potato chips.

And shrimps slathered in mayonnaise.

The girl was singing "Misty".

He closed his eyes again.

I get misty,

she sang,

just holding your hand...

Suddenly, he felt like crying.

It was true.

Yes, it *was* true.

Even after all these years, he *did*, he *did* get misty. Not that there weren't other parts of her he'd like to hold, and much more frequently. But sometimes still—after dinner, say, when the kids were in bed, and they strolled up in the twilight towards the yellow bloom of the corner-store window for an ice cream or an Oh Henry bar, along the sidewalks black where the sprinklers were arcing, under the deepening green mounds of the maples, past the squall and chirping of sparrows roosting behind the Virginia creeper on the side of St. Andrew's Church—sometimes still he'd hold her hand shy and happy as a boy.

He shifted his chair further from the table, crossed his legs. Banged his knee.

Straightened the rucked tablecloth.

The girl was singing.

the way you sip your tea...the memory of all that...

Nothing *could* take away from him the things they'd shared, the way they'd become. The way she worried he'd be struck by lightning via metal street-lights, the way she unpacked grocery boxes on the front porch to prevent the entry of mythical cockroaches, the way she poked with a broom handle because of miners' lung disease, parrots, psi-something, whatever it was called, poking with a broom handle attempting to dislodge nesting pigeons from the upper windows' gingerbread—the list was endless, part of life's fabric, a ballad without end. And this morning? What had been this morning's contribution? Goldfish!

White strings.

In which case, that being so, which it unarguably *was*, what, just *what* was he doing in this ridiculous restaurant with this—*ordinary*. With this very *ordinary* girl? What was he doing with a girl who was nearly young enough to be his daughter? *Was* young enough to be his daughter. With a girl who was only—he calculated—was only—good God!—*five years older than Peter*!

What was he doing with a girl whose silences were abrasive, whose conversation was boring? Who spoke of 'getting into' things? What was he doing with a girl who'd never heard of Jacques Tati? With a girl in whose hands he'd once seen an historical romance, tartan and claymores, entitled *The Master of Stong*? What was he doing with a girl who transported her toiletries in an army-surplus bag?

He stared at it where it hung from the back of her chair.

The writing in gilt on the hairbrush handle glinted.

Pinned to the front of the bag was a black and white button that said:

GRAVITY SUCKS

Behind her head, the movement of figures on the dance floor.

The brightly lighted stage.

Knife and fork.

She looked up and smiled.

With sudden and startling clarity, the realization came to him that she wasn't her at all. *She simply wasn't her.* Polly, he realized, was Polly but Norma wasn't.

But Polly...

What of Polly? What was she?

He sat thinking about that.

T he waitress was mouthing something. Leaning forward and peering up at her face from about eighteen inches away, he watched her lips moving.

He pointed at his ear and shrugged.

He traced on the low tabletop a figure 5 and a zero. Her lips seemed to shape: 50?

She disappeared into the gloom.

The noise was hurting his eyes.

Beside him on the banquette sat a pair of lovelies whose hair was shaved off to a line an inch or so above the ears; above that, it was cut the same length all the way round so that it sat on their heads like caps. They reminded him of the mushrooms in *Fantasia*. Of collaborators. Of a boy called Gregory who'd had ringworm. Light glanced off the skulls, off the shiny, pallid skin. The girl was drenched in obnoxiously cheap perfume which was beginning to make him feel nauseated. Under the shiny skin, a vein crawled. Her escort was naked to the waist save for red-and-white suspenders.

From behind the amplified drummer, lights like lightning flick-flickered flick-flickered. He began to fear induced epilepsy. On the dance floor in front of the stage, shapes heaved and cavorted in the stuttering light. Some were running-on-the-spot. Some seemed to be miming log-rolling. Others were leaping erratically as though to avoid bowling balls being launched at their ankles.

One of the guitarists was wearing ear-mufflers of the kind worn by ground crews at airports.

The Iron Guard looked much like all the other sneering degenerates who adorned the record albums littering Peter's room—sexually ambivalent, grubby, *used*.

The banquette itself was vibrating. The amplified white-plastic violin which had started up was making his teeth ache. Its sound was demented. He could feel vibration deep inside his body; his very organs were being shaken loose.

Norma had described The Iron Guard as being 'main-stream'; he could not imagine the sound of something she'd consider avant-garde. The word 'mainstream' made him think of 'midstream', of the tests he'd undergone after his heart-thing, of his kidneys vibrating.

The waitress plonked down two bottles of Labatt's Fifty Ale and two wet glasses, took his proffered ten-dollar bill, and disappeared into the fug. He felt Norma's breath on the side of his face as she shouted something. He smiled back then stopped because smiling seemed to intensify the pain in his teeth.

Now and again, he caught a few words bellowed by the lead degenerate...

MIS-ER-*RY*

AS YOU ALL CAN *SEE*...

A large pink bubble was swelling from the mushroom girl's blank face. She and her mushroom consort looked, he thought, as if they'd been used for medical experiments.

He wondered if they found each other sexually attractive; he wondered if they would breed.

He was feeling very tired and very old.

He wished, more than anything, that he was at home in the silent kitchen with a peanut butter sandwich, a glass of milk, three Aspirins, and a new issue of *African Arts*, the only sound the occasional scrabble of the basement mouse.

Outside the Château Laurier, and before the taxi, he had not been able to think of any kind and plausible way of excusing himself but now, oppressed by guilt and toothache, he decided that he would leave—the advancing hour—as soon as the beer was finished and the band had executed another number. If this monstrous and outrageous noise was indeed divided into 'numbers'.

It seemed more than possible that it just went on.

Despite his severe pangs of guilt, despite his realization that Polly wasn't Norma, or, more clearly, that Norma wasn't Polly, and despite his welling love for Martha, it was, at the same time, undeniably flattering that Norma felt attracted to a man with drooping pectorals and four white hairs on his chest. But flattering as it *was*, he almost winced as he thought of the way the evening *could* have turned out. He dwelt for a few moments on the compounding horror of an embroilment with a child-woman and employee. He blessed his blind and stupid luck that had preserved him from laying hot hands on her essentials.

Surveying his behaviour over the course of the evening, he could not recall having responded in any way, verbally or physically, that had in any sense committed him. His responses had, he believed, been sufficiently ambiguous. It was she, amazingly enough, who had made all the running. He had not really stepped over the line. Legs under tables could, he decided, be looked on merely as friendly contiguity. Bridges intact, retreat was possible.

Caught in an extraordinary storm, a pleasant evening with a charming young employee of whom he was fond. A few comments tomorrow about how pleasant it had been, up past his bedtime, a matter of taste, of course, but this sweating hellhole perhaps better suited to the younger generation...

Harrumph!

Major Hoople.

That was the stance.

Avuncular.

The harem pants stretched over her long thighs, she was leaning back on the banquette with her feet up on the ledge beneath the table. He looked at her pale toes.

She *was* attractive, of course, impossible to deny, but he saw that it was the attractiveness of a kitten or a puppy, the charm of a filly in a summer field. A matter of sentiment and aesthetics. He appreciated her, he decided, much in the way that he appreciated a painting or a carving.

No.

That had some truth in it but it was not *strictly* true.

He thought of the glycerine-drenched inner parts of ladies which greeted him in the corner-store every time he went to buy a quart of milk.

Fantasy.

That seemed the essential point to hold onto.

Surreptitiously, he tried to lick off the back of his hand the blue heart and arrow the doorkeeper had stamped him with.

A change in the noise was taking place. To the continuous-car-crash effect was being added a noise which sounded like the whingeing of giant metal mosquitoes. The mushroom girl was gawping, a bubblegum bubble deflated on her lower lip. And then the white-plastic violin capered into high gear and the lead degenerate, bent double for some reason, started moaning and bellowing again and Paul realized that the whole thing was still the

MIS-ER-*RY*

AS YOU ALL CAN *SEE*

recitative *still* going on but possibly, he dared to hope, ending.

There was a long-drawn-out crescendo of appalling noises — noises of things under dreadful tension snapping and shearing, of tortured metal screeching, of things being smashed flat, crushed, ripped apart, ricocheting—and then, suddenly, silence.

The crowd's applause, wild whistles, and rebel yells sounded by comparison soft and muted as the shush of waves on distant shore.

He could scarcely believe it had stopped.

He extended his wrist and watch towards Norma and tapped the watch-face.

He mouthed: Let's go.

"What?"

"Sorry."

"Go?" she said.

"It's late. I need my beauty sleep."

"But we've only just got here."

He stood up.

He wanted to be on the other side of the padded doors before The Iron Guard grated again into gear. Sound was coming to him oddly as it sometimes did during the descent into an airport; the inside of his head felt as though it had been somehow *scoured*.

The set of Norma's body suggested disgruntlement.

They threaded their way through the hairstyles and vintage clothing and he heaved open one side of the heavy doors. It was immediately easier to breathe. The tiny foyer was ill-lighted and tiled white like a public washroom. The concrete stairs rose steeply to the door that led out onto the sidewalk.

He was still trying to think of something to say which

would be suitably old-dufferish, avuncular, and affable and which would set the tone for their parting, and, more to the point, for their meeting again in the morning, when the street door above them banged back against the wall and the narrow doorway was jammed by three struggling figures in black. The two outer figures were manoeuvring a central, drooping figure.

As Paul and Norma stared up at these noisy shapes looming over them, the nearest stumbled on the first step. He let go of the central figure to save himself. The central figure slumped to one side pulling the other supporting figure off balance and then, as if in slow motion, fell forward. A yell was echoing. Rubbery, more or less on his feet, gaining momentum, his body hit the handrail, caromed off to hit the wall, bounced off the wall turning somehow so that he was tumbling backwards, windmill arms, hit the rail again. Reflex pushed Paul forward and the figure landed against his chest and arm. He staggered back under the impact.

"Fuck*inankle*!" screamed a voice on the stairs.

Paul was staring down at the face of his son.

"Peter!

"Peter! Are you hurt? *Peter*!"

His face was white and his eyes were closed.

"Who is it?" said Norma.

"Come on! Peter!

Someone belched.

"What happened to him?"

"Oh, good evening, Mr. Denton."

It was the one in his twenties who wore things suspiciously like blouses.

"What *happened* to him?"

"Do you mean," said Norma, "it's *your* Peter?"

Paul lowered the body to the tiled floor and knelt beside him. He quickly checked arms and legs. Felt round the back of his head. Nothing was obviously broken.

"For Christ's sake, what *happened* to him?"

"Is it?" said Norma. "Peter?"

"Well, I lost my balance, Mr. Denton, and he..."

"I *know* you lost your balance, you fucking dimwit. I want to know what happened to him *before.*"

Peter groaned and opened his eyes.

His head rolled.

He seemed to be staring at Norma.

"Peter? Hey, Peter!"

He was trying to say something.

Bent over him, trying to peer at his pupils in the uncertain light, Paul could scarcely believe the obvious: it was not concussion; it was not hypoglycemia; it was not cerebral edema; it was booze. The boy reeked of booze. He felt suddenly weak and shaky; he could still hear the terrifying sound the boy's head would have made as it hit the tiled floor.

He stared up at—Deet, was it? Wiggo? Or was this the one that sounded like something from *Sesame Street?*

He was regarding Paul and Peter owlishly.

As Paul stared at him, he wrinkled his upper lip and nose and sniffed moistly. He wiped his nose on his sleeve.

Paul shook his head slowly.

"Jesus Christ!" he said. *"Je-sus Christ!"*

"Paul?" said Norma. "Is he okay?"

Paul got slowly to his feet.

With both hands, he smoothed back his hair.

He lowered his head and massaged the muscles in his neck.

"Norma," he said, looking up, "I'm sorry, but I'm going to have to ask you to excuse me. I think it'd be better if you left me to deal with this."

"Oh," she said. "You mean..."

"I'd like to talk privately to these..."

He gestured at Wiggo and at the other character who was sitting on the steps.

"Well," she said. "Umm...okay."

"I'll talk to you in the morning."

She hitched up the strap of the army-surplus bag.

"I'm sorry," said Paul.

"Well," she said, "thank you for dinner."

Paul nodded.

Her sandals slapped up the echoing stairs.

At the top of the stairs, she looked down and said,

"Well, goodnight, Paul."

The push-bar door clanged shut behind her.

"*Now*", said Paul. "Let's start again. Wiggo, isn't it?"

"It's Munchy, Mr. Denton."

The one who worked in the Speculative Fiction bookstore,
the one Peter had said was into Tolstoy.

"Munchy, then. Listen carefully, Munchy. I am going to
ask you a question. Where has Peter been and what happened
to him?"

"We were in my apartment, Mr. Denton."

"*And?*"

"Listening to tapes."

"You were in your apartment and you were listening to
tapes—I haven't got all night, Munchy."

He could feel the pounding of his heart, the dryness in his
mouth. It would have been a release and a pleasure to have
thumped this pair until stretchers were necessary. He felt
pressure at his temples and behind his eyes, thought of tubes
contracting, pictured pink things swelling. He took a deep
breath and held it.

Munchy was groping about in his pockets.

"Pay attention! I'm *talking* to you!"

"I'm sorry, Mr. Denton. Have you got a Kleenex?"

Peter was stirring on the floor, groaning. Paul glanced
down at him. Then stared. He was drawing his knees up to his
body. His exhalations were becoming harsh and noisy. Red-
tinged saliva was drooling and spindling from the corner of
his mouth. It was beginning to pool and glisten on the
white tiles.

Quickly, Paul knelt beside him.

"Did he fall before? Was he hit or something? A car?"

Munchy shook his head.

"Did he hurt himself *before* he fell downstairs?"

Munchy shook his head.

"*Answer me!*" shouted Paul. "Can't you see he's bleeding? What kind of friends *are* you? He's bleeding and he's bleeding *internally. What happened to him?*"

They stared at him.

"He didn't," said Munchy.

"Jesus Christ!" said Paul. "Go! Just go! Go and phone for an ambulance."

"*No, no,* no," said the other creature, shaking his head emphatically.

"What do you mean, *no?*"

Pointing at Peter, he said,

"Issribena."

Paul stared at him. The hair was bleached to a hideous chemical yellow and he was wearing a combination false-nose-and-spectacles. His T-shirt was imprinted with the word: Snout.

"It *is*, Mr. Denton," said Munchy. "That's what it is."

"Is *what?*"

"*Issribena!*" said the one on the steps.

"What," said Paul, "is *it?*"

"Ribena," said Munchy.

Paul wondered if The Iron Guard had done something permanent to his head.

He said:

"Say that again."

"Ribena?" said Munchy.

"Yes. What do you mean, 'Ribena'?"

"It's black-currant juice."

"Ribenasafruit," added the creature with the chemical hair.

Paul knelt again and smeared his finger through the slimy, red-tinged spittle. He smelled it. It immediately made him feel queasy.

He got slowly to his feet.

The Iron Guard sounded through the padded doors like the throb of industrial machinery.

Brushing the dust off his pants, he said,

"Ribena, eh?"

"It isn't bleeding, Mr. Denton."

"No," said Paul. "And Ribena did this to him, did it, Munchy?"

Munchy shook his head.

"It didn't?"

"Grover put rum in it."

Paul nodded slowly.

"*That* is Grover?"

There didn't seem much point in trying to talk to Grover. He was engrossed in trailing his fingertips backwards and forwards along the concrete step.

"But *you* didn't drink much of it."

"Well, I don't use it, Mr. Denton. I'm not really into alcohol."

Paul closed his eyes.

He breathed, consciously.

After a few moments, he said,

"Do you know how old Peter is?"

Munchy nodded.

"Speak to me, Munchy."

"Pardon?"

"Tell me. In words."

"Peter?"

Paul nodded.

"Fifteen?"

Paul nodded.

"Well?" he said. "Do you have anything to say?"

Grover was making automobile noises.

Munchy snuffled.

Paul stared at Munchy.

Staring at Munchy, at his eczema, at his safari shirt over which he wore a broad belt in the manner of Russian peasants, at his tux pants and what looked like army boots, the words 'diminished responsibility' came into Paul's mind. Munchy was the sort of character who'd be sentenced to months of community service for drug possession and who'd genuinely find emptying bedpans a deeply meaningful learning experience; interrogating him was like wantonly tormenting the Easter Bunny.

Munchy wiped his nose on his sleeve again.

Paul looked down at Peter and sighed.

He felt immensely weary.

Above the door that led out onto the sidewalk the EXIT sign flushed the white tiles red.

"It's the pollen," said Munchy.

"What?"

"In the season, I always suffer with it."

He pointed at the tip of his nose with his forefinger.

"Or sometimes," he added, "just with environmental dust."

"Munchy," said Paul, "SHUT. UP. Do you understand?"

Munchy nodded.

"Right. Good. Now get hold of his other arm."

Munchy pushed his glasses higher on the bridge of his nose and stooped.

"And Munchy?"

The glasses flashed.

"Don't speak to me!"

Munchy nodded.

"Just don't speak to me!"

I t was drizzling, a thin mist of rain. There were few people on the streets. Paul had hoped that the torrential storm would have cooled and rinsed the air but it was still close and muggy. Peter's head hung. His legs wambled from sidewalk to gutter; his legs buckled; his legs strayed. Most of the passing couples averted their eyes. Supporting him was like wrestling with an unstrung puppet.

Back wet with sweat, Paul propped him against a hydro pole. It was not when he was moving but when he stopped that he felt the pounding of his heart, that his hot clothes clung, that the sweat seemed to start from every pore. The boy felt so thin, his chest like the carcass of a chicken; it amazed Paul that such frailty could weigh so much.

Leaning against Peter to jam him against the pole, Paul stared across the road unseeing, his clumsy tongue touching the dry corrugations of his palate. The muscles in his shoulders ached. Pain stitched his side. He did not seem able to breathe deeply enough.

A lot of girls in a passing car yelled cheerful obscenities.

His eyes followed the ruby shimmer of their rear lights in the road's wet surface.

Stapled to the hydro pole above Peter's head was a small poster advertising a rock group. The band's name seemed to be:
BUGS HARVEY OSWALD

He changed his grip on the boy's wrist and stooped again to take the weight.

Lurching on, he began to set himself goals: as far as the gilt sign proclaiming Larsson Associates: Consultants in Building Design and Research; as far as the light washing the sidewalk outside the windows of the Colonnade Pizzeria; as far as the traffic lights; as far as the next hydro pole.

And the next.

When he reached Elgin Street, he stood propping Peter at the curb waiting for the traffic lights to change. Further up the street, someone in a white apron was carrying in the buckets of cut flowers from outside Boushey's Fruit Market; knots of people were saying noisy good-nights outside Al's Steak House; a couple with ice-cream cones wandered past; he realized that although it felt much later it must just be approaching midnight. He stood staring across Elgin into Minto Park, into its deepening shadows beyond the reach of the street-lights.

It was quiet in the deserted park; the surrounding maple trees seemed to soak up the noise of the traffic. The wet green benches glistened. The houses along the sides of the square looked onto the park with blank windows. Paul felt somehow secluded, embowered, as though he were in an invisible, airy, green marquee. Just before the shadowed centre of the park with its circular flower-bed, the path widened and there stood the large bronze bust. The bust sat on top of a tall concrete slab which served as a pedestal. Before lowering Peter to a sitting position on its plinth, Paul glanced up at the massive head, the epaulettes, the frogging on the military jacket. Against the bank of moonlit cloud behind, the head stared black and dramatic.

Peter sat slumped with his back against the slab.

Paul rearranged the boy's limbs.

The drizzle had stopped; the sky was breaking up. He began to hear the short screech of nighthawks.

He worked his shoulders about and stretched. His legs felt trembly. He thought of quenching his thirst with a quart of Boushey's fresh-squeezed orange juice but imagined Peter's body being discovered in his absence by a dog-walker, imagined sitting in the back of the summoned police car giving chapter and embarrassing verse.

The cuffs of his shirt were sticking to his wrists.

Beyond the central flower-bed was a drinking-fountain.

Two of the four lamps had burned out, their white globes dull and ghostly.

Zinnias. Zinnias and taller pink flowers whose name he didn't know.

His footsteps echoed.

He drank deeply at the fountain and splashed water on his face.

He walked back slowly to the bust. Around at the front of it Peter was invisible but audible, groaning exhalations. Paul bent forward and peered at the bronze plaque bolted into the back of the pedestal.

April 19, 1973
The Embassy of Argentina presents this bronze to the City

of Ottawa as a symbol of Canadian-Argentine Friendship
Mayor of Ottawa
Pierre Benoit
Ambassador of Argentina
Pablo Gonzalez Bergez

Paul walked around the plinth. Peter had not moved. He leaned close to the pedestal to read the plaque above the boy's head. It was darker on this side, the bulk of the bust and pedestal blocking most of the light from the two lamps, and he had to angle his head to make out the words.

GENERAL JOSE DE SAN MARTIN

Hero of the South-American Independence
Born in Argentina on Feb. 25, 1778
Died in France on Aug. 17, 1850
He ensured Argentine Independence, crossed the
Andes and liberated Chile and Peru

Sirens.
Sirens on Elgin Street.
Ambulance.
Silence sifting down again.
Crunching up two tablets of Nikoban gum, Paul stood looking down at Peter. The drizzle had wet his hair and purple food-dye had coloured his forehead and run in streaks down his face. Pallor and purple, he looked as if he'd been exhumed.
Paul sat down beside him on the plinth.
"Peter?
"How are you feeling now? Feel a bit better?
"Peter! Listen! Are you listening? I'll tell you what we're going to do. We'll stay and rest here for a while and let you get sobered up a bit. If your mother saw you like this neither of us'd ever hear the end of it. Come on, now! Sit up! You'll feel a bit better soon.
"Okay? Peter?"
Peter mumbled.
"What? What was that? *You're* tired! And what? You don't

feel very well. No. I can imagine. You're a lucky boy, you know. Do you realize that? It was an amazing coincidence I happened to be in that place tonight. It was the first time I'd ever been there and I can assure you that it was also the last. That *violin*! Christ! It was like root-canal work. If that's the kind of place you hang out in, it's a wonder to me you aren't stone deaf. But you're lucky, Peter. It could have turned out differently. You could have hurt yourself badly on those stairs. You might have been in the hospital right now with your skull smashed. You think about that."

"*ohhhhhhhh*," said Peter.

"Yes," said Paul, "you think about it."

He cleared his throat.

"Norma and I—you saw Norma, didn't you? Norma who works for me? You met her once, I think. It was pure chance that I—that we—were there. As I said before. We'd been having dinner after work with a guy who's got some masks for sale and after dinner he wanted to go on and listen to some music—you know, visiting fireman sort of stuff—tedious really—and Norma'd heard of that place so that's where we ended up."

Paul again glanced at Peter.

"Fellow from Edmonton."

Peter seemed to be studying his kneecap.

"And it was your good luck we did. End up there.

"Even if you hadn't hurt yourself on the stairs, the police would have picked you up. Imagine that? And Munchy and that other creep wouldn't have been much use to you either. Christ! What a pair! One pissed and the other congenital. You ought to have a think about those beauties, Peter. *Real* friends wouldn't have let you get like this. But can you imagine it? You know how she gets. Your mother down at the police station? In the middle of the night? In full flow?

"Anyway, you're safe. That's the main thing. I don't intend to go harping on about this. I just want you to think about it. That's all. Think about what *might* have happened. Okay?"

"*ohhhhhhhh*," said Peter.

"Yes," said Paul, "well, that's what happens when you drink Ribena."

He leaned back against the pedestal listening to the screech of the invisible nighthawks. The cries grew louder and then diminished, fading, grew harsher again as the birds swept and quartered the sky above.

"It's strange, really," he said. "I was just thinking about it. About that club and that abominable bloody music. Know what I was thinking about? It hadn't really occurred to me before. And perhaps it should have. But when *I* was your age I used to drive *my* parents mad with the stuff *I* listened to. Of course, with me it was jazz records. To hear my mother on the subject—well, you know what your grandmother's like— you'd have thought it was Sodom and Gomorrah and the papacy rolled into one. And it didn't help, of course, that most of them were black.

"Oh, I've had some memorable fights with her in my time. She was sort of a female Archie Bunker, your grandmother. Backbone of the Ladies' Orange Benevolent Association. A merciless church-goer. She refused to listen to the radio on Sundays till she was about sixty-five. Yes, in the days I'm talking about your grandmother was a woman of truly *vile* rectitude.

"I remember one time up at the cottage—one summer—I hated it up there when I was about your age. Every day—every single day—she used to bake bread on that old wood stove. Can you imagine? In that heat? It was all just part of her summer campaign to make life unbearable and martyr herself. And piss my father off. But when I was about your age, that summer ...

"I'd only got a few records. I can see them now. 78s, of course. And an old wind-up gramophone. Benny Goodman and Artie Shaw and Ellington and Count Basie. Buddy de Franco.

"I used to sit out there on the porch—it wasn't screened in those days—I used to sit out there playing them over and over

again. 'Take the A Train' and 'Flying Home'. And she could
have *killed* me. When *she* listened to music—and she didn't
really *like* music—she used to listen to a dreadful unaccom-
panied woman called Kathleen Ferrier singing some damn
thing called 'Blow the Wind Southerly'. A very horrible experience, my boy. And if it wasn't that, it was the other side.
'Weel May the Keel Row'. Which was, if possible, worse. You
don't know what suffering *is*.

"But the stuff *I* played was like waving a red flag. Getting
up late and not eating a proper breakfast and then refusing to
swim and just sitting, sitting listening to that…to that…And
off she'd go about vulgarity and nigger minstrels and why
couldn't I listen to something decent like John McCormack
and then *I'd* say that Benny Goodman was not only white but a
respected classical musician and then it'd get worse and her
face red with rage and it'd swell into all decency fled from
modern life and girls flaunting themselves shamelessly and
listening to that concatenation of black booby-faces …well,
you can imagine what it was like. You know how easy it is to
get her started. Though she's mellow now compared with the
way she used to be. All that business over Jennifer's shorts last
year. About their indecency? Remember that?

"Anyway. What I'm getting at is that maybe when you get a
bit older you forget—I don't mean *you*—you, Peter—I mean
one. One forgets what one was like oneself. *That's* what I'm trying to say. Understand? And I'm trying to say that I don't
want to be towards you the way your grandmother was to me.

"What?"

"*nerrrrrrr*," said Peter again.

"No? No you don't want me to be?"

"*nrrrrrrr*," said Peter.

"Now," said Paul, "I'm not saying I could ever *like* the
music you like because, in all honesty, I couldn't. And I don't
want to lie to you. But certainly I ought to be able to tolerate
it. Because I don't want something like taste in music to come

between us. There'd be something...well...so *petty* about that, wouldn't there?"

Peter said nothing.

His head was back against the pedestal and he seemed to be staring up into a maple tree. Paul got to his feet and stood looking down at him.

"Wouldn't there, Peter? Be something petty about that? And that's something that, well...you know, as we *are* talking, it's something we ought to talk about. I know it isn't *just* the music. It's everything the music *stands for.* I realize that. And whatever you might *think*, I *do* understand, Peter, because that's what jazz used to stand for. For me, I mean. When I was fighting with *my* father and mother. It meant the same kind of thing that punk or new wave or whatever you call it means now. But I'll tell you what I resent. What I resent is this being cast in the role of *automatic* enemy. *I'm* not Society. *I'm* not The Middle Class. I'm *me.* A person. Just like you're a person.

"And *I've* got feelings, too.

"Okay?"

Paul stood looking down at Peter's bowed head.

"Look!" he said, beginning to pace. "We've been having a pretty hard time lately, haven't we? Always arguing and squabbling about one thing or another. Getting on each other's nerves. And it's been making me very unhappy, Peter. But you know, for my part, I only criticize you because I want you to grow up decently and become a kind and considerate person. I don't *enjoy* fighting with you. Believe me. But think of it this way. If I *didn't* care about you and love you—care about what you're going to become—and care very deeply—I wouldn't bother with you, would I? It'd be much easier just to ignore you, let you go to hell in a handcart. It'd be a lot easier for me just to shrug my shoulders, wouldn't it?

"But I don't do that, Peter.

"And I think, really, that you *know* why I don't.

"Don't you?"

Paul sat down on the plinth again and turned to face Peter. Peter had not moved. Paul looked at him and then looked down at his shoes. A breath of wind shuddered the leaves in the maple trees and drops of rain-water pattered down on the concrete path.

"I don't know, old son. It's a funny business—the way things work out—and I don't make much claim to understand it. I suppose we all just blunder along doing the best we can, just hoping for the best but...*this* thing—you and me, I mean—it's all so *ridiculous*.

"Peter?"

Paul put his hand on Peter's arm and then shook him gently.

"What? Yes, *I know* you're tired. What? Yes, soon. We'll go home soon. But listen! Let's get this thing thrashed out. I was saying how ridiculous it was, this constant squabbling about things. I mean, it wasn't so long ago that you went everywhere with me. I couldn't even go to the store for a packet of cigarettes without you tagging along. And remember how we used to go fishing every weekend? Just you and me? Remember that? All those sunfish you used to catch? Remember that day a racoon ran off with our package of hotdogs? And those water snakes you used to catch? Revolting damned things! I used to be quite scared of them. You didn't know that, did you? You thought I was just pretending. And remember that day you made me hold one and it vented all that stuff on my hands and shirt? And how it stank? You thought that was *very* funny.

"Remember, Petey?

"So what I'm getting at is that although we've been getting on each other's nerves a bit lately, you can't just wipe out the past. You can't just ignore...well, what it amounts to, most of your life. I guess we're just stuck with it, aren't we? Wretched thing that I am, I'm your father. And you're my *son*, Petey. So I guess..."

"*nrrrnnnnnnnn.*"

"What?"

Peter leaned forward and, without apparent effort, gushed vomit.

Paul jumped up and out of range.

Peter sat staring ahead, his mouth slightly open.

Threads of drool glistened from his lips.

"Peter?"

Paul passed his hand in front of the boy's face. He did not blink; he did not stir.

"*Peter!*"

Paul stared down at him, astounded.

"You ungrateful little *shit*! You're the next best thing to unconscious, aren't you? You selfish little turd! You haven't heard a single goddamned word I've been saying to you, have you? I've been wasting all these pearls of wisdom on the desert air, haven't I? Hello? Hello? Anyone in there? *Peter*! YOUR FATHER IS TALKING TO YOU.

"Nothing, eh?

"The motor's run down, has it?

"Ah, well...

"I suppose it makes a change, though. Your not answering back. I ought to be grateful, really. You've got a mouth on you like a barrack-room lawyer. Always arguing the toss, aren't you? Black, white. Day, night. Left is right and vice versa. I ought to be grateful for brief mercies. I've daydreamed sometimes of having myself surgically deafened.

"You're always bleating about social justice and revolution —and look at you! Purple hair and vintage puke-slobbered clothing. Let me tell you, my little chickadee, that any self-respecting revolutionary would shoot you *on sight*. Thus displaying both acumen *and* taste.

"Some revolution you'd run. You and Munchy and Bunchy and Drippy and Droopy. What would you do after you'd liberated Baskin-Robbins?

"That's a nice touch. Doing your face purple as well. Suits you.

"Neat but not gaudy.

"And to revert for a moment to the subject of music. You, my dear boy, and your fellow-members of The Virgin Exterminators, are about as much musicians as is my left bojangle. You'd be hard put to find middle C under a searchlight. Musically speaking, blood of my blood and bone of my bone, you couldn't distinguish shit from shinola.

"Hello?

"Yoo-hoo!

"Anyone at home?

"*You're an offensive little heap*! What are you? 'I'm an offensive little heap, Daddy.' Yes, you are! And you're also idle, soft, and spoiled. And in addition to that, you've spewed on my shoe.

"What do you imagine's going to happen to you? Who the hell's going to hire you when you leave school? For what? What can you *do*? You can't even cut the lawn without leaving tufts all over the place. And dare I ask you to trim the edges with a pair of shears? You were outraged, weren't you? 'By *hand*!' you said. How do you think *I* do it? By foot? Wanted me to buy one of those ludicrous buzzing machines to save your poor back from stooping. And when you've chopped it to pieces so that it looks as if you've gone at it with a knife and fork, you have the nerve to demand two bucks. It's all so easy, isn't it?

"Just shake the old money tree.

"Well, life isn't like that, my little cherub. Life isn't a matter of rolling out of your smelly bed at eleven in the morning and lounging around sipping Earl Grey tea and eating nine muffins rich in fibre. Life, my little nestling, is tough bananas.

"And what are you doing to prepare yourself for its rigours? Studying hard? Mastering your times-tables? Practising the old parlez-vous? Getting a grip on human history? History! Dear God! Stone hand-axes, the Magna Carta, the Pilgrim Fathers—it's all the same sort of thing, isn't it? Events that took place in that dim and inconceivable period before the Rolling Stones. The glories of civilization—it's all B.S., isn't it?

"Before Stones.

"And math? You don't even know your tables. Oh, I'll admit you're very handy with the calculator on that fancy watch of yours but I'm afraid *you'd* have to admit that you'd be up the well-known creek if the battery gave out.

"In sum, then, you're close to failing in damn near every subject. And why is that? What was the reason you advanced? Something about school being 'a repressive environment'. I'm not misquoting you, I hope. And what was it you received a commendation in? A discipline I hadn't encountered before. 'Chemical Awareness', I believe it was called.

"In which you have now moved on, I see, to practical studies.

"Pissed out of your mind at fifteen.

"What mind you have.

"And speaking of pissed, and I apologize for bringing this up, as it were, when you're a little under the weather, but I'd be gratified if you could remember in future to raise the toilet seat before relieving yourself.

"I mention this because I am tired of living knee-deep in balled Kleenex, soiled underwear, crusted piss, and rotting tofu.

"I am, as a matter of fact, tired of a hell of a lot of things.

"Oh!

"Yes.

"I also wish you'd shave your upper lip every couple of weeks now you're nearing man's estate. You look like a spinster with hormonal imbalance.

"And another matter of petty detail.

"That cat.

"I don't like it.

"That cat is going back to the SPCA *forthwith.* To be humanely electrocuted to death IN A WET STEEL BOX."

Stooping and grabbing up a rotten branch which had fallen in the storm, Paul beat it against the trunk of the nearest maple until it shattered into fragments. He threw the pieces, one by one, as far as he could out onto the grass. He threw them with all the power and violence he could command. He threw them until his elbow joint began to hurt.

He turned and walked back towards the pedestal. The pool of vomit between Peter's feet glistened. He sat on a nearby bench and spread his arms along the back.

He crossed his legs.

He breathed in deeply and then sighed profoundly.

He stared up at the great bronze bust of San Martin.

"*Well?*" he demanded of the moonlight touching the high military collar, the frogging, the starburst of a military decoration or royal Order.

"What do you say, José? How was it with you? What do *you* have to offer? You wear your seventy-two years easily, I'll say that for you. You have that calm and peaceful look about you of the man who gets laid frequently. I'd lay odds *you* didn't live in an open-plan house.

"It's about all I *can* lay.

"Odds.

"And what about *Mrs.* José De San Martin? Doubtless a beauty, you salty dog. Veins surging with hot southern blood? Bit of a handful? I don't suppose *she* had to go out to work. Wasn't too tired at night? Wasn't worrying that the children might hear? That the tomato chutney in the basement might explode?

"Lucky man, José.

"And the kids? I expect they were tucked up in their nursery half a mile away in the East Wing?

"And *not* by you.

"Very sensible, too.

"And she adored you?

"Well mine adores me but she's got a lot on her mind. Is the gas turned off? Did she or didn't she put Tooth Fairy money under Jennifer's pillow? Will chutney attract rats? It takes the bloom off it, José.

"But I've always been faithful to her. Up till tonight, that is.

"What happened? That's a good question, José. I wish I knew. There's this girl, you see. Polly Ongle. And...well, I *wasn't* unfaithful. Though I could have been. Or maybe *not*. No. There's a thought. Maybe not. And anyway, this one turned out to be Norma. To tell the truth, I'm a bit confused about it, José. You see, I'm beginning to suspect it was all about something else.

"Can I put it more clearly? I'm not surprised you ask.

"No.

"But you. These campaigns of yours. When you were away from her. I expect you rogered your way across the continent. I don't suppose you went short of a bit of enchilada, did you? Oh, don't misunderstand me! I'm not being censorious. If anything, I'm envious, José. It's just that it isn't so simple now. A lot of other things have been liberated since Chile and Peru.

"I wish I'd flourished then.

"It seems more vivid, somehow. Somehow simpler.

"Jingling home after you'd given the hidalgos a severe thumping about in the course of liberating this or that, clattering into the forecourt of the ancestral home, tossing the reins to one of the adoring family retainers, striding through the hall in boots and spurs,

"'Coo-ee, *mi adoracion*! I have returned! It is I.'

"And then off with the epaulettes, down with the breeches, and into the saddle.

"*Whereas*, José, when *I* return—granted not from a two-year campaign but from a two-day business trip—there's no question of skirts up and knickers joyfully down. I have to suffer a lengthy interrogation about expenditures on my Visa card.

"Following which she promptly collapses.

"Why, you ask?

"Because, José, for two nights she has not slept. She has not slept because she has lain awake, José, worrying (a) that I might have been killed in any of an astounding variety of ways and (b) that the burglars and perverts who surround my house would take advantage of my absence and kill *her*.

"After first buggering, of course, all the children.

"Talking of which, how did yours turn out?

"Children, I mean.

"A comfort to you in your old age? A source of pride? Or did they cause you grief? Blackballed from clubs? Welshed on debts of honour? Or did they rally round bringing Dad his cigar and nightly posset?

"Tell me, José, what would *you* have done with *this*? Head under a pump and a stick across his back, eh? It's an attractive thought. Very attractive. But he'd have me up in front of the Children's Aid soon as look at me. Probably argue his own case, too. With *his* mouth, he wouldn't *need* a lawyer. And I'd end up being forced to increase his allowance and buy him a colour TV.

"The army? Well, these days I'm afraid they don't take all comers. They tend to ask questions. Such as what's five multiplied by twelve. And I don't suppose they'd let him use his watch.

"I don't know, José. This one's bad enough. But I've got two more coming to the boil. What are *they* going to dream up to break my heart? Need I ask? I *know*. In the middle of the night, I *know*. My little daughter will get herself tattooed and fuck with unwashed, psychotic bikers. My other son will blossom suddenly queer as a three-dollar bill. What does one do? What does one *do*?

"You lived a long time, José."

Close ranks and face the front.

"Well, there's a gem from the military mind. *Very* comforting. But forgive me. I'm being rude. I'm forgetting. You *do* know more about fortitude than I do. I'd forgotten that. Was it a daily bitterness? All your titles resigned, your honours returned. Thirty-odd years, wasn't it? In France? Thirty-some years in voluntary exile. And all in support of a monarchy nobody wanted.

"I don't know, José.

"But on the other hand, it couldn't have turned out worse than generals in sun-glasses.

"Was it worth it, José? Looking at it now? I've never been there. Argentina. Used to read about it when I was a kid. Gauchos deadly with knife and bola. That sort of thing. But if the rest of the world is anything to go by, the gauchos are probably wired to Sony Walkmans and the pampas is littered with Radio Shacks.

"Still, you did it when the doing of it was fun. Horses. Gorgeous uniforms and women swooning. South American heart-breakers all looking like Bianca Jagger with flowers in their teeth.

"'Was it worth it?'

"What a stupid question!

"Of *course* it was worth it.

"Before. After. All those years in bitter exile.

"Of *course* it was worth it. Leather, harness, steel, pennons snapping in the wind. For those eight years you were larger than life. Coming down out of the mountains, your columns trailing you, the guns bouncing on their limbers—you were living in a dream. Oh, don't think I don't understand!

"I envy you, José.

"You breathed an air I've never breathed.

"I envy you that, José.

"God! I envy you that.

"'*Was it worth it!*'

"Look at us!

"Here's me down here with puke on my shoes—ever tried to get it off suede?—and there's you up there growing greener every year.

"Ah, well...

"What can you do?

"As my father-in-law, the philosopher, says,

"'What can you do?'

"What can you do, José?

"What can you do, flesh of my flesh?

"No contributions from you?

"No ready answers?

"Good.

"That's a relief.

"Come on, then. Heave! Up you come! Don't *step* in it! Beddy-bye time for you. Come on! That's it. We're going walkies. *Hasta la vista, José.* Come on, Peter. Say goodnight to the General. That's it. Christ, you smell revolting! Get your feet out of the zinnias, there's a good boy. *This* way! This way! Come on! Five more blocks. Walk *straight*! Come on, Petey. You can do it. Five more blocks and then you can sleep. Good! That's it. Good boy. Good boy, Petey.

"Left, right.

"Left, right.

"Not so *much* left.

"Right.

"Steady the Buffs! Steady! Correct that tendency to droop. And get your leg out of that juniper bush. What do you think this is, you 'orrible little man? A nature ramble? Now, then. Close ranks and face the front. *That's* the front—where the street-light is. And on the word of command, it's forward march for us.

"Ready?

"*Forwaaard*—

wait for it!

wait for it!

MARCH."

Single Gents Only

Affter David had again wrested the heavy suitcase from his father's obstinately polite grip and after he'd bought the ticket and assured his mother he wouldn't lose it, the three of them stood in the echoing booking hall of the railway station. His mother was wearing a hat that looked liked a pink felt Christmas pudding.

David knew that they appeared to others as obvious characters from a church-basement play. His father was trying to project affability or benevolence by moving his head in an almost imperceptible nodding motion while gazing with seeming approval at a Bovril advertisement.

The pink felt hat was secured by a hat-pin which ended in a huge turquoise knob.

Beyond his father's shoulder, looking over the paperbacks on the W. H. Smith stall, was a woman in a sari. David kept under observation the vision of the bare midriff and the ponderous hand of the station clock while pretending to listen to the knit-one-purl-one of his mother's precepts.

His father eventually made throat-clearing noises and David promptly shook his hand. He stooped to kiss his mother's cheek. Her hat smelled of lavender, her cheek, or possibly neck, of lily-of-the-valley. He assured her that the ticket was safe, that he knew where it was; that he'd definitely remember to let her know in the letter for which she'd be waiting if the train had been crowded; if he'd managed to get a seat.

The loudspeakers blared into demented announcement

flurrying the pigeons up into the echoing girders. The on-slaught of this amplified gargle and ricochet coincided with his mother's peroration, which seemed to be, from the odd phrase he caught, a general reworking of the Polonius and Mr. Mic-awber material, warnings against profligacy, going to bed late, burning the candle at both ends, debt, promiscuity, not wear-ing undershirts, and drink.

She gripped his hand.

He watched her face working.

As the metal voice clicked silent, she was left shouting, "THE SECRET OF A HAPPY LIFE IS..."

Mortified, David turned his back on the gawping porter.

She continued in a fierce whisper,

"...is to *apportion* your money."

He returned their wavings, watching them until they were safely down into the tiled tunnel which led to the car-park, and then lugged his case over to the nearest waste basket, into which he dropped the embarrassing paper bag of sandwiches.

With only minutes to go before his train's departure, the barmaid in the Great North-Western Bar and Buffet set before him a double Scotch, a half of best bitter, and a packet of Balkan Sobranie cigarettes. Flipping open his new wallet, he riffed the crisp notes with the ball of his thumb. The notes were parchment stiff, the wallet so new it creaked. Smiling, he dismissed the considerable change.

The Scotch made him shudder. The aroma of the Sobranie cigarettes as he broke the seal and raised the lid was dark, strange, and rich. He was aware of the shape and weight of the wallet in his jacket's inside pocket. Stamped in gold inside the wallet were words which gave him obscure pleasure: *Genuine Bombay Goat*. With a deft flick of his wrist, he extinguished the match and let it fall from a height into the ashtray; the cigarette was stronger than he could have imagined. He raised the half of bitter in surreptitious toast to his reflection behind the bar's bottles. Smoke curling from his nostrils, he eyed the Cypriot barmaid, whose upper front teeth were edged in gold.

He sat in a window seat of the empty carriage feeling special, feeling regal, an expansive feeling as physical and filling as indigestion. He crossed his legs, taking care not to blunt the immaculate crease in his trousers, admiring his shined shoes. A mountain of luggage clanked past, steam billowed up over the window, a whistle blew. And then the carriage door opened and a toddler was bundled in from the platform followed by a suitcase and parcels and carrier-bags and its mother. Who hauled in after her an awkward stroller.

Doors slamming down the length of the train.

"Ooh, isn't the gentleman kind!" said the woman to the toddler as David heaved the suitcase up onto the luggage rack.

"And these?" said David.

From one of the carrier-bags, a yellow crocodile made of wood fell onto his head.

The toddler started to struggle and whine as the train pulled out. It was given a banana. It was pasty-looking and on its face was a sort of crust. Old food, perhaps. Possibly a skin disease. It started to mush the banana in its hands.

Turning away, David gazed out over the backs of old jerry-built houses, cobbled streets, cemeteries, mouldering buildings housing strange companies found in the hidden parts of towns visible only from trains: Victoria Sanitation and Brass, Global Furniture and Rattan, Allied Refuse. Clotheslines. The narrow garden strips behind the houses looking as if receding waters had left there a tide-line of haphazard junk.

The train cleared the neat suburbs, the gardens, the playing fields for employees, picked up speed, vistas of distant pit-heads, slag-heaps, towering chimneys and kilns spreading palls of ochre smoke, all giving way to fields and hedges, hedges and fields.

Inside his head, like an incantation, David repeated:

The train is thundering south.

Beside the shape of the wallet in his jacket's pocket was the letter from Mrs. Vivian Something, the University's Accommodations Officer. The tone of the letter brusque. He had not replied promptly as he had been instructed so to do and no vacancies now existed in the Men's Halls of Residence. Nor were rooms now available on the Preferred List. Only Alternative Accommodation remained.

274 Jubilee Street.

The morning sunshine strong, the train thundering south, the very address propitious, *Jubilee.*

As the train bore him on towards this future, he found himself rehearsing yet again the kind of person he'd become. What kind of person this was he wasn't really sure except that he'd known without having to think about it that it wasn't the kind of person who lived in Men's Halls of Residence.

Blasts on its whistle, the train slowing through a small country station.

Nether Hindlop.

On the platform, rolls of fencing wire, wicker crates of racing pigeons, holding a ginger cat in his arms, a porter.

But at the least, he thought, the kind of person who bestowed coins on *grateful* porters. He still blushed remembering how on his last expedition to London he'd tipped a taxi-driver a shilling and the man had said,

'Are you sure you can spare it?'

And later, even more mortifying, after a day in the Tate and National galleries, he had sat next to a table of very interesting people, obviously artistic, in a crowded café in Soho. He'd listened avidly as they chatted about Victor this and Victor that and he'd realized gradually that Victor must be Victor *Pasmore.* And as they were leaving, the man with the earring had paused by his table and said in a loud voice,

'So glad to have had you with us.'

Even though he had been seared with shame and burned even now to think of it, he had in a way been grateful. He admired the rudeness and aggression and the ability to be rude and aggressive *in public*; the realm of books apart, he still considered it the most splendid thing that he had heard another person actually *say*.

But he found it easier to approach what he would become by defining what he was leaving behind. What he most definitely *wasn't*—hideous images came to mind: sachets of dried lavender, Post Office Savings Books, hyacinth bulbs in bowls, the *Radio Times* in a padded leather cover embossed with the words *Radio Times*, Sunday-best silver tongs for removing sugar-cubes from sugar-bowls, plump armchairs.

But *how*, he wondered, his thoughts churning deeper into the same old ruts, *how* did one change from David Hendricks, permanent resident of 37 Manor Way, ex-Library Prefect and winner of a State Scholarship, to something more...more raffish.

'Hold a woman by the waist and a bottle by the neck.'

Yes.

Somerset Maugham, was it?

Not much of a point of etiquette in his own teetotal home, he thought with great bitterness, where wild festivities were celebrated in Tizer the Appetizer and where women were not held at all.

"*Whoopsee!*" cried the mother.

The toddler was launched towards him, was upon him. He looked down at his trousers. He tried to prise the clenched, slimy fingers from the bunched material.

"There," he said, "there's a good boy..."

"Not afraid of anything, *she* isn't!" said the woman proudly.

David blushed.

"Proper little tomboy, encha?"

David smiled.

And regarded his ruined knees.

The house stood on a corner; the front of the house faced onto Jubilee Street, the side of the house faced the cemetery on the other side of Kitchener Street. From the coping of the low wall which bounded the cemetery, rusted iron stumps stuck up, presumably the remains of an ornamental fence cut down for munitions during the Second World War. In an aisle of grass between two rows of tombstones, a small dog bunched, jerking tail, its eyes anguished.

There were no facing houses on the other side of Jubilee; there was a canal, tidal the driver had told him, connecting with the docks. The tide was out. Seagulls screeched over the glistening banks of mud. The smell came from the canal itself and from the massive red-brick brewery which stood on its far side.

Most of the tiny front garden was taken up by an old motor-bike under a tarpaulin.

"*Not* Mr. Porteous?" she said.

"No," said David, "I'm afraid not."

She held the letter down at a distance, her lips moving. Wiry hairs grew on the upper lip. He suddenly blushed remembering that her house had been described as Alternative Accommodation and hoping that she wouldn't be embarrassed or hurt.

Her gross body was divided by the buried string of the grubby pinafore. Her hair was grey and mannish, short back and sides with a parting, the sort of haircut he'd noticed on mentally defective women in chartered buses. The torn tartan slippers revealed toes.

"They didn't mark that down," she said.

"Pardon?"

"About the back double."

"Double?"

"With the Oxford gentleman."

"Oh," said David. "You mean...?"

"Yes," she said. "They should have marked that down."

He manoeuvred his suitcase round the hatstand and bicycle in the gloom of the narrow passage and followed her ponderous rump up the stairs. Reaching for the banister, grunting, she hauled herself onto the dark landing.

Even the air seemed brown.

"This is the bathroom," she said, "and the plumbing."

He sensed her so close behind him that he felt impelled to step inside. The room was narrow and was largely taken up by a claw-foot bathtub. Over the tub, the height of the room and braced to the wall, bulked the monstrous copper tank of an ancient geyser.

She was standing behind him, breathing.

He began to feel hysterical.

The lower part of the tank and the copper spout which swung out over the tub were green with crusty verdigris; water sweating down the copper had streaked the tub's enamel green and yellow. Wet, charred newspaper half blocked the gas-burners in the geyser's insides.

"If you wanted a bath, it's a shilling," she said, slippers shuffling ahead of him, "with one day's warning."

Following her into the bedroom, he stared at the vast plaster elephant.

Two single beds stood on the brown linoleum. The wall-paper was very pink. Pinned on the wall between the beds was a reproduction cut from a magazine of Annigoni's portrait of Queen Elizabeth.

"You can come and go as you please—the key's on a string in the letterbox—but we don't have visitors."

David nodded.

"I don't hold with young ladies in rooms."

"No, of course," said David. "Quite."

His gaze kept returning to the elephant on the mantelpiece. Inside the crenellated gold of the howdah sat a brown person-age in a turquoise Nehru jacket sporting a turban decorated with a ruby.

"Well..." he said.

Staring at him, doughy face expressionless, she unscrewed a Vicks Nasal Inhaler and, pressing one nostril closed, stuck it up the other.

He politely pretended an interest in the view.

Below him, a staggering fence patched with warped ply-board and rusted lengths of tin enclosed a square of bare, packed earth.

There was a bright orange bit of carrot.

On one of the sheets of tin, it was still possible to make out an advertisement for Fry's Chocolate.

In the middle of this garden sat a disconsolate rabbit.

When the sounds seemed to have stopped, he turned back to face the room. He looked round nodding judiciously, aware even as he was doing it that it was the sort of thing his father did. He had, he realized, no idea of how to conclude these negotiations.

"And this other person? The man from Oxford?"

"Mr. Porteous."

"He's...?"

"We had a telegram."

"Ah," said David, "yes. I see."

"Cooked breakfast and evening meal included," she said, "it's three pound ten."

"Well," said David, contemplating the elephant, "that sounds..."

"And I'll trouble you," she said, "in advance."

H e shoved the empty suitcase under the bed.
The thin quilt, the sheets, the pillow, all felt cold and damp.

He thought of turning on the gas fire but didn't have a shilling piece; he thought of putting a sweater on.

Jingled the change in his pocket for a bit, inspected the wallpaper more closely; the motif was lilac blossoms in pink edged with purple. It was five-thirty. He wondered at what time, and where, this evening meal was served, if 'evening meal' meant tea in some form or dinner.

Voices.

Slap of slippers on lino.

He eased his door open a crack.

"*Evening Post*. Now that should serve her nicely, the *Evening*

Post. Six pages of the *Post*. Read the newspaper, do you? Not much of a fellow for the reading. Scars, though! Now that's a different story entirely. Did I show you me scars?"

Through the banisters, an old man's head with hanging wings of white hair. Behind him, a stout boy in a brown dressing-gown.

The boy stood holding a sponge bag by its string; his calves were white and plump.

"Now there's a dreadful thing!" said the old man, who was scrabbling about on his hands and knees with the sheets of newspaper manufacturing a giant spill. "A dreadful thing! Two hundred homeless. Will you look at that! There, look, and there's a footballer. Follow the football, do you? Fill in the Pools? Never a drop of luck I've had. Spot the Ball? But a raffle, now! A raffle. I fancy the odds in a raffle. A raffle's a more reasonable creature than Spot the Ball."

He disappeared into the bathroom.

The front door slammed shaking the house.

Boots clumping.

Then the dreadful voice of Mrs. Heaney.

"PERCY?"

"WHAT?"

"PERCE!"

"Quick, now!" shouted the old man. "Quick! Holy Mother, she's in full flow!"

Matches shaking from the box, he secured one against his chest and then rasped it into flame. He set fire to the drooping spill.

"BACK, BOY! BACK!"

Body shielded by the door, face averted, he lunged blindly. The expanding sheet of light reminded David of war films. The old man's quavering cry and the explosion were nearly simultaneous.

Brown shoulders blocking the view.

Suddenly from below, at great volume, Paul Anka.

I'M JUST A LONELY BOY...

The old man was in the smoke stamping on the spill.
Ash, grey and tremulous, floated on the air.

In front of Mrs. Heaney's place at the head of the table stood
a bottle of Cream Soda.

The kitchen was silent except for the budgerigar ringing its
bell and stropping itself on the cuttlefish. The cooked evening
meal was a fried egg, a wafer of cold ham, a quarter of a
tomato, and three boiled potatoes.

The slice of ham had an iridescent quality, hints of green
and mauve.

In the centre of the oilcloth stood Heinz Ketchup, Crosse
and Blackwell's Salad Cream, HP Sauce, Branston Pickle, OK
Sauce, Daddy's Favourite, A1 Sauce, a bottle of Camp Coffee,
and a punctured tin of Nestlé's Evaporated Milk.

Sliced white bread was piled on a plate.

The old man bobbed and fidgeted darting glances.

The fat boy was called Asa Bregg and was from Manchester
and had come to university to study mathematics. Ken, who
had acne and a Slim Jim tie and lots of ball-point pens, was an
apprentice at Hawker-Siddeley. Percy, presumably Mrs.
Heaney's son, glimpsed earlier in overalls, was resplendent in a
black Teddy-boy suit, white ruffled shirt, and bootlace tie.
What forehead he had was covered by a greasy elaborate wave.
He was florid and had very small eyes. The old man was
addressed as 'Father' but David was unable to decide what
this meant.

Cutlery clinked.

Percy belched against the back of his hand.

The old man, whose agitation had been building, suddenly
burst out,

"Like ham, do you? A nice slice of ham? Tasty slice of ham?
Have to go a long way to beat..."

"Father!" said Mrs. Heaney.

"...a nice slice of ham."

"*Do you want to go to the cellar!*"

Cowed, the old man ducked his head, mumbling.

The budgerigar ejected seeds and detritus.

David studied the havildar or whatever he was on the label of the Camp Coffee bottle.

Mrs. Heaney rose heavily and opened four tins of Ambrosia Creamed Rice, slopping them into a saucepan.

Percy said,

"Hey, tosh."

"Pardon?" said David.

"Pass us the slide."

"Pardon? The what?"

Percy stared.

"Margarine," said Ken.

"Oh! Sorry!" said David.

Crouched on the draining-board, the cat was watching the Ambrosia Creamed Rice.

The old man, who'd been increasingly busy with the cruet, suddenly shouted,

"Like trains, do you? Interested in trains? Like the railway, do you? Fond of engines?"

"*Father!*"

Into the silence, Asa Bregg said,

"*I* am. I'm interested in trains. I collect train numbers."

The old man stared at him.

Even Percy half turned.

Ken's face lifted from his plate.

Asa Bregg turned bright red.

"I'm a member of the Train-Spotters Club."

Alone in the room that was his, David stared at the plaster elephant. He wondered how they'd got the sparkles in.

After the ham and Ambrosia Creamed Rice, he'd walked the neighbourhood—dark factories across the canal, bomb-sites, news agents, fish and chips, Primitive Methodist Church, barber, The Adora Grill, and had ended up in the Leighton Arms where in deepening depression he drank five pints of the stuff manufactured opposite his room, an independent product called George's Glucose Stout.

The pub had been empty except for an old woman drinking Babycham and the publican's wife, who was knitting and listening to *The Archers*.

At the pub's off-licence, as a gesture of some kind, he'd bought a bottle of cognac.

He arranged on top of the chest of drawers the few books he'd been able to carry, the standard editions of Chaucer and Spenser serving as bookends, and settled himself on the bed with Cottle's *Anglo-Saxon Grammar and Reader*. Skipping over some tiresome introductory guff about anomalous auxiliary and preterite-present verbs and using the glossary, he attempted a line of the actual stuff but was defeated by the conglomeration of diphthongs, thorns, and wens; he had a presentiment that Anglo-Saxon was not going to be his cup of tea.

Heavy traffic up the stairs, voices, a strange jangle and clinking. Mrs. Heaney appeared in the doorway and behind her a tall man with blond hair.

"This is Mr. Porteous," she said, "from Oxford."

"David Hendricks."

"How do you do? Jeremy Porteous. If I could trouble you?" he said, handing the tightly furled umbrella to Mrs. Heaney. He dropped the canvas hold-all on the floor and, slipping off the coiled nylon rope and the jangling karabiners and pitons, tossed them and the duffle coat onto the bed.

He glanced round.

"Splendid," he said. "Splendid. Now, in the morning, Mrs. ...ah...Heaney, isn't it? ...I think, *tea*."

"About the rent, Mr. Porteous."

"A matter for discussion, Mrs. Heaney, if you'd be so kind, following breakfast. I've had rather a gruesome day."

And somehow, seconds later, he was closing the door on her.

He smiled.

"There's a person downstairs," he said, "called 'Father'. Seemed to want to know, rather insistently, if I enjoyed travelling by bus."

David grinned.

Advancing on the gas-fire and elephant, Jeremy said, "There's a special name, isn't there, for this chocolate chap? The one on its neck?"

"Mahout," said David.

Seemingly absorbed, Jeremy moved back a pace the better to view the elephant. He had a slight limp, David noticed, and was favouring his right leg.

"Pardon?" said David.

"'A plate'," repeated Jeremy, "'of Spam'."

David wondered how it was possible to wear a white shirt in combination with an anorak smeared with mud and at the same time look as suave as the men in the whisky advertisements.

"What are you going to..." David hesitated "...read at university?"

"Actually," said Jeremy, "I'm supposed to be involved in some research nonsense."

"Oh!" said David. "I'm terribly sorry. I just assumed... What did you do at Oxford?"

"I spent the better part of my time," said Jeremy, still intent on the elephant, "amassing an extraordinarily large collection of photographs of naked eleven-year-old girls with their ankles bound."

David stared at the elegant back.

He could think of absolutely nothing to say.

The gas-fire was making popping noises.

Desperate to break the silence, David said,

"Have you been climbing? Today, I mean?"

"Just toddling about on The Slabs at Llanberis. Are any of these free? I really must rest these shirts."

As he wrestled open a drawer in the chest, the mirrored door of the wardrobe silently opened, the flash of the glass startling him.

"Did you hurt your leg today?" said David, embarrassed still and feeling it necessary to ease the silence. "When you were climbing?"

"I hurt it," said Jeremy, dropping on his bed toothpaste, toothbrush, towel, and a large green book, "not minutes ago, and quite exquisitely, in what is probably referred to as the hall. On a sodding *bicycle.*"

He added to his toiletries a pair of flannel pyjamas decorated with blue battleships.

"Good God!" he said, pulling back the quilt, patting further and further down the bed. "This bed is positively *wet.*"

"Mine feels damp, too," said David.

"*Yours* may be damp," said Jeremy. "*Mine* is *wet.*"

He hurled the rope and the climbing hardware into a corner.

"Wet!" he shouted, striking the bed with his furled umbrella, "*Wet! Wet! Wet!*"

He seemed almost to vibrate with rage.

He pounded on the lino with the umbrella's ferrule.

"*Can you hear me, Mrs. Heaney? Are you listening, you gravid sow?*"

He stamped so hard the room shook and the wardrobe door swung open.

"WET!"

He glared about him.

He snatched at the string between the beds.

It broke.

With a loud *clung,* the gas-meter turned itself off.

He stood beside the bed with his eyes closed, one arm still rigid in the air holding the snapped string as though he were miming a straphanger in the Underground. Light glinted on the gold and onyx cuff-link. Slowly, very slowly, he lowered the arm. Opening his fingers, he let the length of string fall to the floor. Eyes still closed, he let out his pent breath in a long sigh.

He limped over to the window. He swept aside the yellowed muslin curtains. He wrenched the window high. He limped to the mantel. He hurled the elephant into the night.

David realized that he, too, had been holding his breath.

The edges of the curtains trembled against the black square.

David cleared his throat.

"Would you," he said, reaching under the bed, "would you like a drink?"

"Ummm?" said Jeremy, turning, wiping his hands with a handkerchief.

"A drink?"

"Ah, brandy!" said Jeremy. "Good man! It might help in warding off what these beds will doubtless incubate. Sciatica, for a start."

"Lumbago," said David.

"Rheumatoid arthritis," said Jeremy.

"*Mould*," said David.

Jeremy laughed delightedly.

Digging into his hold-all, he came up with a black case that contained telescoping silver drinking cups which, with a twist, separated into small beakers. He caught David's expression and said,

"Yes, a foible, I'm afraid, but I've always been averse to the necks of bottles. Equal in the eyes of God and all that sort of thing, certainly, but would one share one's toothbrush? Well, bung-ho!"

Along the rim of the beaker, David saw the shapes of hallmarks.

"'Lumbago'," said Jeremy. "Don't you find that certain words make you think of things they don't mean? 'Emolument', for example. Makes me think of very naked, very fat, black women. Something I read as a stripling about an African king's wives who were kept in pens and fed starchy tubers—so fat they couldn't get up—just rolled around—and *oiled* all over, rather like..." his hands sketched a shape "...rather like immense *seals*...What was I starting to say?"

"Lumbago," said David.

"Yes," said Jeremy. "I wonder why?"

There was a silence.

"So!" said Jeremy.

David nodded.

Jeremy held out his cup.

"What are you going to do?" said David.

"In the morning," said Jeremy, "we shall fold our tents. What was that woman called?"

"Mrs. Heaney?"

"No. The lodgings woman."

"The Accommodations Officer?"

"*She's* the one. Cornbury? Crownbury? We shall proceed against her."

"But I thought—well, from her letter, that there *wasn't* anywhere else."

"Nonsense."

"Are you just *allowed* to leave a...?"

"*Who*," demanded Jeremy, "who got us into this—this *lazarhouse* in the first place? The responsibility is purely hers. We shall question her judgment with indignation and bitterness."

"But..."

"With *voluble* indignation and bitterness. We shall demand reparations. *Silver*," he said, "is so comforting to the touch, isn't it?"

David held up the brandy bottle.

"Well," said Jeremy, "*yes.*"

"But you see..." said David.

"See what?"

"I paid her a week's rent."

"Always," said Jeremy, "try to *postpone* payment. On the other hand," he said judiciously, "never bilk."

"Well," said David, "now that you've...I mean, she's not likely to return my..."

"Life," said Jeremy, climbing into his pyjama bottoms, "is very much a *balancing*, a trading-off of this against that. It's a simple question, surely? The question is: Are you the sort of person who lives in a place like this? To which," he said, working a khaki sweater down over his pyjama top, "one hopes there can be but one reply."

He reassembled the bed and spread his duffle coat over the quilt and on the duffle coat spread two sweaters and his rope.

"I find sleep impossible," he said, "without *weight*."

Whistling "We Plough the Fields and Scatter", he went out with toothbrush and towel.

David sat on the bed enjoying the brandy, enjoying the weight and balance of the silver cup, savouring Jeremy's use of the word: *we*. Thinking about the amazing fluctuations of the long day, he decided that the flavour of events was exactly caught in the casual connective of biblical narrative: *And it came to pass...*

The wallpaper made him feel as if he were sitting inside a friendly pink cave.

He was, he realized, drunk.

Jeremy returned whistling the hymn about those in peril on the sea and started to work himself under the layers of bedding. He asked David to pass him the book, a large paper edition of *The Wind in the Willows* with illustrations by Ernest Shepard.

"I say," said Jeremy. "Would you...I mean, would it be a terrible imposition?"

"Would what?"

"Just to read a few paragraphs?"

"I haven't read this," said David, "since I was a child."

"Oh, but you should!" said Jeremy with great earnestness. "It never lets you down."

"From the beginning?"

"No," said Jeremy. "Let me think. Oh, this is *lovely*! There's the field mice singing carols to Ratty and Mole at 'Mole End' — that's always very nice. But...*I* know! Let's have the part where Ratty and Mole go to visit Toad. Remember? Where the motor-car wrecks Toad's caravan? Yes, here it is."

He passed over the book.

He closed his eyes, composed his hands.

"Most kind of you."

David began.

The old grey horse, dreaming, as he plodded along, of his quiet paddock, in a new raw situation such as this simply abandoned himself to his natural emotions. Rearing, plunging, backing steadily, in spite of all the Mole's efforts at his head, and all the Mole's lively language directed at his better feelings, he drove the cart backwards towards the deep ditch at the side of the road. It wavered an instant —then there was a heart-rending crash—and the canary-coloured cart, their pride and joy, lay on its side in the ditch, an irredeemable wreck...

Toad sat straight down in the middle of the dusty road, his legs stretched out before him, and stared fixedly in the direction of the disappearing motor-car. He breathed short, his face wore a placid, satisfied expression, and at intervals he faintly murmured "Poop-poop!"

The Mole was busy trying to quiet the horse, which he succeeded in doing after a time. Then he went to look at the cart, on its side in the ditch. It was indeed a sorry sight...

The Rat came to help him, but their united efforts were not sufficient to right the cart. "Hi! Toad!" they cried. "Come and bear a hand, can't you!"

David, turning the page, glanced over at Jeremy. His eyes were closed, his breathing deepening.

"Glorious, stirring sight!" murmured Toad, never offering to move. "The poetry of motion! The real way to travel! The only way to travel! Here today—in next week tomorrow! Villages skipped, towns and cities jumped—always somebody else's horizon! O bliss! O poop-poop! O my! O my!"

"O stop being an ass, Toad!" cried the Mole despairingly.

"And to think I never knew!" went on the Toad in a dreamy monotone.

David looked up.

With a long sigh, Jeremy had turned on his side.

His breathing deepened into a snore.

The coiled rope was balanced on the hump of his shoulder.

"All those wasted years," David continued, reading aloud in the pink bedroom, "that lie behind me, I never knew, never even dreamt! But now—but now that I know, now that I fully realize! Oh what a flowery track lies spread before me, henceforth! What dust-clouds shall spring up behind me as I speed on my reckless way!"

Jeremy's exhalations were a faint, breathy whistle.

David closed the book.

The edges of the curtains trembled against the black square of the open window.

He switched off the light.

He pulled the quilt up to his chin and lay in the darkness listening.

Somewhere far distant in the night, in the docks perhaps, perhaps slipping its moorings and preparing to move out down the river to the sea, a ship was sounding and sounding.

The Eastmill Reception Centre

After a year in the university's Department of Education, a year worn thin discussing the application of Plato to the Secondary Modern School and enduring my tutor, a mad dirndl woman who placed her faith in Choral Speaking, this was to be my first taste of the real world.

While Uncle Arthur was assembling a ring of the necessary keys, I stood looking down from his office window into the asphalt quadrangle where the boys were lounging and smoking, strolling, dribbling a football about. They all wore grey denim overalls and black boots.

"The wife and I," said Uncle Arthur, "were not blessed with issue."

I turned and nodded slowly.

"So in a sense—well, the way *we* feel about it—every last one of these lads is *our* lad."

I nodded and smiled.

Uncle Arthur was short and tubby and was wearing grey flannels and a grey sleeveless pullover. Strands of fine blond hair were trained across his reddened pate. He looked jolly. In the centre of the strained pullover was a darn in wool of a darker grey. It drew attention like a wart.

"Here's your keys, then. They're all tagged. And use them at *all* times. Artful as a barrel-load of monkeys, they are, and absconders is the *last* thing we want. One whistle with lanyard. There's your timetable. And a word of advice, a word to the wise. If you get yourself into difficulties, just you come to me. I'm House Father and it's what I'm here for. Comprendo?"

"Thanks," I said. "I'll remember that."

"Right, then..." said Uncle Arthur.

I glanced at my timetable.

"*Gardening?*"

"Oh, everyone takes a hand at gardening," said Uncle Arthur. "Very keen on gardening, the Old Man is. Doesn't know you're here, does he? The Old Man? You didn't phone from the station?"

"No," I said. "Was I supposed to?"

"Probably wiser," said Uncle Arthur, "yes, to wait till morning."

I nodded.

"*Mid*-morning," he added.

I looked at him.

"A nod's as good as a wink," he said, "if you get my drift."

"Oh, right," I said. "Of course."

"That's the ticket!" said Uncle Arthur. "Well, you come along with me, then, do the evening rounds, get the hang of things."

I followed him along the disinfectant- and polish-smelling corridor, down the echoing steel stairs, out into the warmth of the summer evening.

Pallid faces, cropped hair, army boots. I was the centre of much obvious speculation. I kept close to Uncle Arthur and endeavoured to look bored. I nodded as casually as I could at the faces which stared most openly.

We mounted the steps of the North Building. Uncle Arthur blew one long blast on his whistle and all motion froze. His glance darted about the silent playground.

"Nothing like a routine," he murmured, "to settle a lad down."

Two blasts: four boys ran to stand beneath us, spacing themselves about ten feet apart.

"House Captains," explained Uncle Arthur.

Three blasts: the motionless boys churned into a mob and

then shuffled themselves out into four lines. He allowed a few seconds to elapse as they dressed ranks and then blew one long blast.

Silence was rigid.

As each boy, House by House, called out *Present, Uncle Arthur!* in response to his surname, Uncle Arthur ticked the mimeographed sheet. When numbers were tallied and initialled, Churchill House and Hanover moved off first to the showers.

"Never initial anything," said Uncle Arthur, "until you've double-checked personally. Best advice I can give you. I learned that in the Service and it's stood me in good stead ever since."

Stripped of their grey overalls, the boys looked even more horribly anonymous, buttocks, pubic hair, feet. I glanced down the line of naked bodies trying not to show my embarrassment and distaste. I looked down at Uncle Arthur's mauve socks in the brown open-work sandals. At the further end of the line, a mutter of conversation was rising. Uncle Arthur's whistle burbled, a sound almost meditative.

"Careful you don't lose your pea, Uncle Arthur," said one of the tallest boys.

All the boys laughed.

"It won't be *me*, lad," said Uncle Arthur, nodding slowly, ponderous work with his eyebrows, "it won't be *me* as'll be losing my pea."

I recognized this as ritual joke.

The laughter grew louder, wilder, ragged at the edges.

Order was restored by a single blast.

He advanced to a position facing the middle of the line.

Into the silence, he said,

"Cleanliness, Mr. Cresswell, as the Good Book says, is next to Godliness. So at Eastmill here it's three showers a day *every* day. We get lads in here that come from home conditions you wouldn't credit. Never had contact with soap and water, some of them. Last time some of this lot touched water was when they was christened. *If* they was christened. *Sewed* into their underclothes, some of them are. And dental decay? Horrible! Turns the stomach, Mr. Cresswell. Athlete's foot. Lice. Scabies and scales. Crabs of all variety. Crabs, Mr. Cresswell, of every stripe and hue."

He surveyed the silent line.

"Start with little things, you see, Mr. Cresswell, because little things lead to big things. That's something that in the Service you *quickly* learn. And talking of *little things*," he bellowed suddenly, his face flushing, "what are *you* trying to hide, lad? *Stand up STRAIGHT!*"

Half turning to me, he said from the side of his mouth,

"A rotten apple if ever I saw one. Attempted rape was the charge. Got off with interference."

I nodded and avoided looking at the boy.

In spite of all the showering, there was a close smell of sweat, feet, sourness.

While Uncle Arthur raked the naked rank with his flushed glare, I made a pretence of reading the mimeographed names on the clipboard. I found myself thinking of the strange civil service gentleman, somehow connected with the Home Office, who'd interviewed me a month earlier.

We like our chaps to have rubbed along a bit with other chaps.

Boxing, eh? The Noble Art, hmm?

Excellent. Excellent.

My role, he had informed me, would be both educational and diagnostic.

Uncle Arthur's keys clinked in the awful silence. He selected one, and the captain of Churchill stepped out of line to receive it. The boy unlocked a metal cupboard and took out a square ten-pound tin and an aluminum dessert spoon.

Upon command, the boys began to file past holding out a cupped hand and Uncle Arthur spooned in grey tooth-powder.

"Better than paste," he confided. "What's paste but powder with the water added?"

The boys were crowding round the racks of tagged tooth-brushes, bunching round the six long sinks, dribbling water

onto the powder, working it up in their palms with the brushes.
"What about the others?" I said. "The other boys?"

"They'll be at their exercises in the yard with Mr. Austyn.
In the quadrangle. Stuart House and Windsor tonight.
Anyone who goes on report, you see, the whole House suffers.
Ginger them *all* up. Doesn't make the offenders popular. Dis-
courages them as likes to think of themselves as hard cases."

A scuffle was starting around the last sink. The sounds of
hawking, gobbing, gargling, were becoming melodramatic.

"Right! Let's have you!" bellowed Uncle Arthur. "Lather
yourselves all over paying special attention to all crevices
—and no skylarking!"

He turned on the showers and the dank room filled with
steam. The pale figures slowly became ghostly, indistinct.
Conversation was difficult above the roar of the water.

When the showers were turned off, the boys dried themselves, fixed the soggy towels round their waists, and formed a
single line facing the far door. Uncle Arthur unlocked the door
and the line advanced. The first boy stopped in front of us,
stuck his head forward, contorted his features into a mocking
grimace. I stared at him in amazement, fearing for him. Uncle
Arthur inspected the exposed teeth and then nodded. Face after
snarling face, eyes narrowed or staring, flesh-stretched masks,
until the last white towel was starting up the stairs.

"Here's a tip for you just in passing," said Uncle Arthur as
he double-locked the door and we followed them up, "a
wrinkle, as you might say, that they wouldn't have taught you
in the university. Tomorrow, in the morning showers, keep
your eyes skinned for any lad as has a tattoo. Right? Then you
have a read of his file. Right? Any young offender, as they're
now called, any young offender that's got a tattoo, you be on
the *qui vive* because sure as the sun shines you've got trouble on
your hands. Right?"

I nodded.

"Most particularly," said Uncle Arthur, stopping, puffed by
the stairs, "if it says 'Mother'."

There were forty beds in the dormitory, twenty on each side of the room. On each bed was a single grey blanket. Hanging from the end of each iron-frame bed was a grey cloth draw-string bag. The boys, now in pyjamas, stood at attention at the foot of the beds.

Uncle Arthur surveyed them.

Then nodded.

The boys opened the cloth bags, taking out rolled bundles of *Beano* and *Dandy, Hotspur, Champion,* and *The Wizard.*

"Providing there's no undue noise," said Uncle Arthur, "comics till nine."

I followed him down the sounding stairs and along another blank corridor until he stopped and said,

"Here we are, then—our home away from home."

The Common Room contained six shabby Parker-Knoll armchairs, two coffee tables, and a low bookcase stacked and heaped with pamphlets and old newspapers. In one of the armchairs sat a morose middle-aged man whose spectacles were wrapped at the bridge with a Band-Aid. By the side of his chair stood a wooden crate of beer. He was wearing slippers, his feet stretched out towards the electric fire where imitation flames flickered.

"Mr. Grendle," said Uncle Arthur, "our metal-work teacher. Our new English teacher, Mr. Cresswell."

"How do you do?" I said.

Mr. Grendle did not look up and did not reply.

"Well..." said Uncle Arthur.

The yellowing muslin curtains stirred in the breeze.

"Coffee," said Uncle Arthur, "tea," pointing to an electric kettle and some unwashed cups and spoons. "Ale you'll have to organize for yourself."

Mr. Grendle tapped out his pipe on the arm of the chair, swept the ash and dottle onto the floor, wiped his palm on his cardigan.

"Perhaps," said Uncle Arthur, "you'd better come along and see your room, get yourself settled in."

"*A scriber!*" said Mr. Grendle, staring at the imitation flames. "A scriber in the back. Or battered with a ball-peen hammer. That's how *I'll* end."

As we went out into the fading light of the summer evening, Uncle Arthur said,

"Get's a bit low, sometimes, does Henry. Since his accident."

"Accident?"

"Yes," said Uncle Arthur. "That's right. Now this is a view I've *always* been partial to."

We stood looking at the screen of trees, at the long gravel drive which turned down through tended lawns and shrubs to the Porter's Lodge, a single-storey brick building beside the gate in the tall mesh fence which was topped by angled barbed-wire.

Far below us, a man was wandering over the lawns spiking up scraps of paper.

"Often comes out for a constitutional around this time," said Uncle Arthur.

"Pardon?"

"The Old Man."

The figure disappeared behind a clump of rhododendrons.

"Well," said Uncle Arthur, consulting his watch, "no rest for the wicked, as they say. Time for me to relieve Mr. Austyn. Now over *here's* where you are, in the West Building."

My room was featureless. A red printed notice on the inside of the door said: Please Keep This Door Locked At All Times. On the iron-frame bed were two grey blankets. I hung up clothes in the small varnished wardrobe, stacked shirts and underwear in the varnished chest of drawers, stowed the suitcase under the bed. I set my small alarm-clock for six-thirty.

The toilet paper was harsh and stamped with the words: Not For Retail Distribution.

Lying in bed under the tight sheets, I found myself thinking of the boys in the dormitory, found myself wondering if the serials *I'd* read as a boy were still running in the comics, the adventures of Rockfist Rogan, the exploits of Wilson the Amazing Athlete. Was it *Hotspur* or *The Wizard?* I could feel the rough paper, smell the smell of the paper and print. I found myself wondering if the Wolf of Kabul with his lethal cricket-bat bound in brass wire was still haunting the Frontier.

And as I drifted into sleep, I remembered the name of the cricket-bat. The Wolf of Kabul. He'd called it 'Clickee-baa'.

Tick-tock of the clock.

Clickee-baa.

W hen I entered the Staff Dining Room next morning with my tray, one of the two men at the long table called,

"Do come and join us! Austyn. With a 'Y'. Sports and Geography."

He was tall and boyish, dressed in a white shirt and cricket flannels.

"My name's Cresswell," I said, shaking his hand, "and I'm supposed to be teaching English."

"And my surly colleague," he said, "is Mr. Brotherton. Woodwork."

I nodded.

"You're a university man, I understand?" said Mr. Austyn as I unloaded my tray. "Something of a *rara avis* in Approved School circles."

"Oh, I'm just a novice," I said.

"I, myself," he said, "attended Training College. Dewhurst. In Surrey."

Mr. Brotherton belched.

"Well, look," said Mr. Austyn, rising, draining his cup, consulting his watch in a military manner, "time marches on. I'd better be getting my lads organized. I'll look forward to talking to you later."

I watched him as he walked out. He was wearing white plimsolls. He walked on his toes and seemed almost to bounce.

Mr. Brotherton explored his nose with a grimy handkerchief and then started to split a matchstick with his horny thumbnail.

I drank coffee.

He picked his teeth.

"'I *attended* Training College'!" he said suddenly.

"Pardon?"

"I've 'attended' a symphony concert at the Albert Hall but it doesn't mean I played first sodding violin."

"What do you mean by that?"

"You wouldn't likely think it," he said, getting to his feet and tossing a crumpled paper napkin onto the table, "but I was once a sodding cabinet-maker."

In the quadrangle, the boys, lined up House by House, were standing silent but at ease facing the steps of the North Building. It was five minutes to eight. Uncle Arthur and Mr. Austyn were supervising two House Captains who were positioning on the top step a record-player and two unhoused speakers. Uncle Arthur adjusted the height of the microphone stand. Not knowing what exactly to do, I sat on the low wall by the side of the East Building.

The microphone boomed and whined. One of the House Captains touched the needle of the record-player and a rasp sounded through the speakers. Mr. Grendle hurried out of the East Building bearing large plywood shields. He propped them against the low wall beside me and hurried back into the building. The outer shield said: STUART. A man I hadn't seen before strode up and down the lines rearranging a boy or two here and there to establish an absolute descending order of height.

Uncle Arthur looked at his watch.

He blew a single blast.

In a long shuffle of movement, the boys dressed ranks.

Mr. Austyn said something urgently to Uncle Arthur and Uncle Arthur turned to one of the House Captains, jabbing his finger in my direction.

The boy sprinted towards me.

"Is it these you want?" I said, fumbling together the awkward sliding shields.

"Oh, fucking hell!" said the boy, grabbing them from me, nearly dropping them, bumping me in his urgency.

"*Ssssst!*" said a voice behind me.

Turning, I saw Mr. Grendle on top of the East Building steps urging me in clenched pantomime to stand at attention.

Mr. Brotherton, his face expressionless, stood sentry on the top step of the South Building.

The whistle shrilled again; the boys stiffened; the shields, HANOVER, STUART, WINDSOR, and CHURCHILL, were steadied by the captains. Mr. Austyn lowered his outstretched arm as though applying a slow-match to a touch-hole. At this signal, the crouching boy lowered the needle onto the record. There was a loud preliminary hissing before the music rolled forth. The awful volume and quality of sound brought to mind fairgrounds and gymkhanas. Uncle Arthur held wide the North Building's heavy door. The brass and massed choir worked their way through "Land of Hope and Glory".

Nothing happened.

The crouching boy put on another record.

The National Anthem blared.

At

Long to reign over us

the shadowed doorway darkened and a large man in a brown suit walked out past Uncle Arthur and stood before the microphone. His chest was massive. He seemed almost without a neck. He was wearing mirrored sunglasses. Stuck at the angle of his jaw was what looked like a small piece of toilet-paper. What could be seen of his face was red and purple.

As the Anthem concluded, the boy lifted off the hissing needle.

Our Father Which Art in Heaven
Hallowed Be Thy Name
said the Headmaster.

And stopped.

The silence extended.

And extended.

Mr. Austyn was quivering at attention.

The Headmaster cleared his throat. The head moved, the mirrored lenses scanning the four ranks.

"If I find a boy," he said slowly, his voice heavy with menace, "*not* pulling together, I'm going to be very sorry for that boy. Very sorry indeed. But not half as sorry as that boy is going to be."

There was another long silence.

He brought out a packet of cigarettes and a box of matches and looked down at them and then put them back in his jacket pocket.

He then buttoned the jacket.

Uncle Arthur moved to his side and the microphone picked up the murmured prompting.

Thy Kingdom Come...

"What do you say, Arthur?" boomed the microphone.

The head and torso turned ponderously to the left; he seemed to be staring at the shield that said WINDSOR.

For ever he suddenly said *and ever. Amen* and his brown bulk broke from the microphone and strode past the taut white figure of Mr. Austyn into the shadows of the doorway and disappeared.

Roll-call followed.

Followed by morning showers.

My classroom was less than a quarter the size of a normal classroom and the twenty boys were jammed along the benches. There was somewhere, Uncle Arthur believed, a set of readers. I issued each boy with a sheet of paper and a pencil, and, as I had been instructed by Uncle Arthur, wrote on the blackboard:

When I grow up, I want to—

These papers were to be read by Dr. James, described by Uncle Arthur with a wink and a finger pressed to the side of his nose as 'the old trick cyclist'.

I watched the boys writing, watched the way the pencils were gripped or clasped. I curbed the use of the wall-mounted pencil-sharpener after a couple of boys had managed to reduce new pencils to one-inch stubs. I denied nine requests to go to the lavatory. At the end of the allotted time, I collected and counted the pencils and glanced through what Uncle Arthur had called the 'completions'.

They were brief, written in large, wayward script, and violent in spelling. Some of the papers were scored almost through. Deciphered, they expressed the wish 'to be pleeceman', 'to hav big musels', 'to go Home', etc.

One paper was blank except for the name sprawled huge.

"Who's Dennis Thompson?"

A boy put up his hand. He looked about eleven or twelve.

"Why didn't you complete the sentence, Dennis?"

"Well, I don't do writing, do I?"

The accent was south London.

"Why's that?" I said.

"Well, I'm excused, aren't I?"

"Excused?"

Uncle Arthur bustled in. I was to meet the Old Man. Immediately. The boys were left with dire threats. I was hurried through the North Building and out of the rear door. The brown-suited figure was standing some two hundred yards distant with his back to us looking at the vast area given over to garden.

"Word to the wise," puffed Uncle Arthur, laying his hand on my arm, "sets great store, the Old Man does, by being called 'Headmaster'."

As we drew nearer, Uncle Arthur cleared his throat.

The Headmaster's hand was large and moist.

Uncle Arthur was dismissed.

The Headmaster returned to his contemplation of the large floral bank which spelled out:

EASTMILL RECEPTION CENTRE

I stood beside him looking at the greyish plants of the

lettering, the green and red surrounding stuff.

"The letters," he said, after a long silence, "of the display are Santalima Sage. A hardy perennial."

I nodded.

"The red," he said, pointing, "the green, the contrasting foliage, known as the filler, is called Alternamthera."

I nodded again and said,

"It's extremely impressive, Headmaster."

"A tender annual," he said.

"Pardon?"

"Alternamthera."

"Ah!" I said.

"I am proud of our record here at Eastmill, Mr. Cresswell. In eleven years, *three—*"

The mirrored glasses were turned upon me.

"—only *three* absconders."

I nodded slowly.

"Two," he said, "were caught before they'd gone five miles." He paused.

"The third was apprehended in Pontypool."

There was a long silence.

We studied the floral display.

Eventually, he cleared his throat in a manner which I took to be a sign that the interview was concluded.

"Thank you, Headmaster," I said.

The long day bore on with three more 'completions', lunch supervision, midday roll-call and showers. The cricket match between Windsor and Stuart with twenty boys on each side was interminable. The shepherd's pie and jam-roll with custard weighed upon me. Uncle Arthur, seemingly tireless, drove the boys on through the afternoon's hot sun. An occupied boy, he held, was a happy boy. As we stood joint umpires at the crease his public exhortations were punctuated by *sotto voce* asides:

"Don't ponce about, lad! Hit it square!"

Stole a Morris Minor.

"Come on, lad! That's not the spirit that won the war!"
Had half a ton of lead off of a church roof.
The game lasted for more than three hours.

After evening meal supervision, roll-call, and evening showers, I settled down in the empty Common Room with the files of those names I'd managed to remember. I'd scarcely got myself arranged, coffee, ashtray, cigarettes, when the door opened and I looked up at a man of about forty who was wearing a blue suit with a Fair Isle pattern pullover.

"Good evening," I said. "My name's Cresswell."

"James," he said, nodding his head almost as if ducking, and then plugged in the electric kettle.

"Not *Dr.* James?"

"Well, not really. It's a Ph.D. You're from a university. I did *try* to explain..."

He came over and sat facing me. The blue shoulders were dusted with dandruff. He began to fiddle with a tiny bottle of saccharine tablets, trying to shake out just one.

"I'm about to make a start on your files," I said.

"Were you interviewed by the Home Office?"

"For this job? I'm not sure really. Some sort of civil service character."

"They *all* call me 'Doc'," he said. "Even the boys."

I watched him trying to funnel saccharine tablets back into the bottle.

"Have you spoken to the Headmaster? Since you've been here?"

"Yes," I said. "This morning."

"Did he by any chance say anything to you about me? In any way?"

"No," I said. "He..."

"Or imply anything?"

He started nibbling at his thumbnail.

"No. He didn't say *anything*, really. Just warned me about boys absconding. He seemed to want me to look at his flower-bed-thing. Actually," I said, "he seemed rather *odd*."

"Odd!" said Dr. James. "*Odd*! The Headmaster—"

He got up and went to close the door.

"Files," he said, guiding the boiling water into his mug, "files and expert opinion are obviously the centre of any such organization as this. The heart. The very core."

He looked up, spectacles befogged by steam.

I nodded.

The teaspoon was stuck to the newspaper.

"The Headmaster," he said, "the Headmaster ignores my reports. He rejects all my recommendations. He deliberately undermines the efforts of all my work. Deliberately. And he openly influences the staff against me."

"Why?" I said.

Seating himself again, he took off his spectacles and stared at me with naked eyes.

"There have been countless ugly incidents. He's incapably alcoholic, but of course you must have realized that. And for all this, accountable to no one, of course, we have the Home Office to thank."

"But why would he undermine your ...?"

"Because he perceives me as a threat."

The naked eyes stared at me. He rubbed the spotty spectacles on the Fair Isle pullover.

"Threat in what way?"

"The man has no education whatever beyond elementary school. Yes! Oh, yes! But there's more you should know, Mr....er ..."

"Cresswell," I said.

"For your own protection."

He peered again towards the door.

"Before he became Headmaster, he was employed—I have access to the files—the man was employed by the City of Eastmill—"

He bent his head and hooked the springy wire side-pieces of the spectacles around the curves of his ears and looked up again.

"—employed as a *municipal gardener.*"

"No!" I said.

He nodded.

"But how on earth..."

"Ask our masters at the Home Office."

"Good God!" I said.

He carried the mug of coffee to the door.

"Mention to no one," he said, "that we have spoken."

I settled down to read.

The files contained condensed case histories, I.Q. scores, vocabulary scores, reports from previous schools, reports from social workers and probation officers, family profiles, anecdotal records, recommendations. The files were depressingly similar.

Thompson, Dennis.

I remembered him, the London boy from the morning who'd claimed to be excused from writing, the waif's face, the dark lively eyes. Fifteen years of age. According to the scores he'd received in the *Wechsler-Bellevue, Stanford and Binet, Terman and Merrill*, etc., his achievements and intelligence were close to non-existent. His crime was arson. Three derelict row-houses in Penge had been gutted before the flames had been brought under control.

He claimed not to know why he had done it.

He said he liked fires.

I soon lost my nervousness of these boys under my charge. As the days passed, I stopped seeing them as exponents of theft, rape, breaking and entering, arson, vandalism, grievous bodily harm, and extortion, and saw them for what they were—working-class boys who were all, without exception, of low average intelligence or mildly retarded.

We laboured on with phonics, handwriting, spelling, reading.

Of all the boys, I was most drawn to Dennis. He was much like all the rest but unfailingly cheerful and co-operative. Dennis could chant the alphabet from A to Z without faltering, but he had to start at A. His mind was active, but the connections it made were singular.

If I wrote CAT, he would stare at the word with a troubled frown. When I sounded out C-A-T, he would say indignantly: Well, it's *cat*, isn't it? We had a cat, old tom-cat. Furry knackers, he had, and if you stroked 'em...

F-I-S-H brought to mind the chip shop up his street and his mum who wouldn't never touch rock salmon because it wasn't nothing but a fancy name for conger-eel.

C-O-W evoked his Auntie Fran—right old scrubber *she* was, having it away for the price of a pint...

Such remarks would spill over into general debate on the ethics of white women having it off with spades and Pakis, they was heathen, wasn't they? Said their prayers to gods and that, didn't they? *Didn't* they? Well, there you are then. *And* their houses stank of curry and that. You couldn't deny it. Not if you knew what you was talking about.

These lunatic discussions were often resolved by Paul, Dennis's friend, who commanded the respect of all the boys because he was serving a second term and had a tattoo of a dagger on his left wrist and a red and green humming-bird on his right shoulder. He would make pronouncement:

I'm not saying that they are and I'm not saying that they're not but what I *am* saying is...

Then would follow some statement so bizarre or so richly irrelevant that it imposed stunned silence.

He would then re-comb his hair.

Into the silence, I would say,

"Right. Let's get back to work, then. Who can tell me what a vowel is?"

Dennis's hand.

"It's what me dad 'ad."

"*What!*"

"It's your insides."

"What is?"

"Cancer of the vowel."

The long summer days settled into endless routine. The violent strangeness of everything soon became familiar chore. Uncle Arthur left me more and more on my own. Showers and the inspection of teeth. Meal supervision. Sports and Activities. Dormitory patrol.

The morning appearances of the Headmaster were predictably unpredictable. The Lord's Prayer was interspersed with outbursts about what would happen if boys did not pull their weight, the excessive use of toilet-paper, an incoherent homily concerning the flotilla of small craft which had effected the strategic withdrawal of the British Army from Dunkirk, and, concerning departures from routine, detailed aphasic instructions.

Every afternoon was given over to Sports and Activities.

Cricket alternated, by Houses, with gardening. Gardening was worse than cricket. The garden extended for roughly two acres. On one day, forty boys attacked the earth with hoes. The next day forty boys smoothed the work of the hoes with rakes. On the day following, the hoes attacked again. Nothing was actually planted.

The evening meals in the Staff Dining Room, served from huge aluminum utensils, were exactly like the school dinners of my childhood: unsavoury stews with glutinous dumplings, salads with wafers of cold roast beef with bits of string in them, jam tarts and Spotted Dick accompanied by an aluminum jug of lukewarm custard topped by a thickening skin.

Uncle Arthur always ate in his apartment with the wife referred to as 'Mrs. Arthur' but always appeared in time for coffee to inquire if we'd enjoyed what he always called our 'comestibles'.

Mr. Austyn, referred to by the boys as 'Browner Austyn', always said:

May I trouble you for the condiments?

Between the main course and dessert, Mr. Brotherton, often boisterously drunk, beat time with his spoon, singing, much to the distress of Mr. Austyn:

> *Auntie Mary*
> *Had a canary*
> *Up the leg of her drawers.*

Mr. Grendle drizzled on about recidivists and the inevitability of his being dispatched in the metalwork shop. Mr. Hemmings, who drove a sports car, explained the internal-combustion engine. Mr. Austyn praised the give and take of sporting activity, the lessons of co-operation and joint endeavour, The Duke of Edinburgh's Awards, Outward Bound, the beneficial moral results of pushing oneself to the limits of physical endurance.

But conversation always reverted to pay scales, overtime rates, the necessity of making an example of this boy or that, of sorting out, gingering up, knocking the stuffing out of etc. this or that young lout who was trying it on, pushing his luck, just begging for it etc.

The days seemed to be growing longer and hotter; clouds loomed sometimes in the electric evenings promising the relief of rain, but no rain fell. The garden had turned to grey dust; cricket-balls rose viciously from patches of bald earth. Someone stole tobacco; there was a fight in the South Building dormitory. Comprehension declined; pencils broke. Showerings and the cleaning of teeth measured out each day.

One afternoon at the end of my fifth week, I was in charge of thirteen boys, seven having been commandeered by Mr. Grendle to do something or other to his forge. At the shrill of my whistle, the boys halted outside Mr. Austyn's shed while I drew and signed for the necessary cricket gear.

I unlocked the gate in the wire-mesh fence, locked it behind us. The cricket bag was unpacked; two boys were detailed to hammer in the stumps. The rest stood in a listless group grumbling about bleeding sunstroke and bleeding running about all bleeding afternoon for bleeding nothing.

There were only three bails; I had signed for four, had watched them go into the bag.

"Bail?" repeated a boy in vacant tone.

"What's he mean, 'bail'?" said another voice.

"It's money what you have to pay to get out the nick."

"You stupid berk!" said another voice.

The laughter grew louder, jeering.

I shrilled on the whistle, confronted them.

"I will give you," I said, "precisely five seconds to produce the missing bail."

"What's he going on about?"

"If the bail," I said, "is *not* produced..."

A flat voice said,

"Oh fuck the fucking bail."

Lunging, I grabbed a handful of the nearest denim, swung the boy off his feet. He fell on one knee. I jolted him backwards and forwards ranting at him, at them.

"*Sir!*"

Dennis's voice penetrated.

"'Ere! Sir!"

The boy fell slack; he was making noises.

My hand was like a claw.

I wandered away from them, crossing the limed line of the boundary, and sat waiting for my heart to stop the thick hammering. The close-mown grass was parched and yellow. Beyond the mesh fence yards in front of me were thick woods a quarter of a mile deep before the beginning of the houses of the East Point subdivision. In the afternoon heat the trees were still. I watched the unmistakable dance of Speckled Wood butterflies over the brambles, dead leaves, and leaf-mould at the wood's dappled edge. As a child, I'd chased them with my green muslin net. I stared beyond them into the darkening, layered shade.

Time had passed without my noticing. The missing bail had appeared; the game had got under way without the usual squabbling; was now winding down to a merely formal show of activity.

Dennis wandered over, and, in a pretence of fielding,

crouched down a few yards away from me.

"It's all right, Dennis," I said.

He nodded. He sat down.

"It's all right," I said again.

Soon all the boys were sprawled in the grass.

"Wish we could play in there," said Dennis, staring into the woods.

I lay back and closed my eyes listening to their voices.

You could make a house in a tree like on the telly. That family. They had this house...

You haven't got no hammer and you haven't got no nails. And you haven't got no bits of old wood neither.

What about Tarzan, then? He didn't have no hammer neither.

Red suns behind my closed eyelids glowed and faded.

'Ere! Know what I'd be doing right now if I was Tarzan? Do you? I'd be having a bunk-up, having a crafty one with Jane.

Get lost! With a face like yours, wanker, you'd be lucky to cop a feel off his bleeding monkey.

I sat up and forced the key around the double ring until it was free. I tossed it to Dennis.

"Be back here," I said, "in one hour. Understand?"

As I lay back in the grass, I heard their yells and laughter, the sounds of their passage through the undergrowth, sounds which grew fainter. Later, a thrush started singing.

At three o'clock, I walked back towards the four main buildings.

Well, even that, I suppose, could do as an ending. Of sorts.

Lacking in drama, some might say.

Pastel colours. Too traditional.

I know all about that.

...marred in its conclusion by an inability to transcend the stylistic manner of his earlier work...

If I were interested in finishing this story, in cobbling it up into something a bit more robust, it's here that I ought to shape the thing towards what would be, in effect, a *second* climax and denouement. It's at this point that I should make slightly more explicit the ideas which have been implicit in the detail and narrative matter, treating them not baldly *as ideas*, of course, but embodying them, in the approved manner, in incident. (As a story-writer, I'm concerned, needless to say, with feelings, with moving you emotionally, not sermonizing.) And what is it exactly, then, that I would wish to emerge a touch more explicitly were I interested in rounding the story off for your entertainment? Certainly nothing intellectually stunning. Platitudes, some might say. That the guard is as much a prisoner as those he guards; that the desire to conform, to fulfil a role, distorts and corrupts; perhaps, to extend this last, that the seeds of Dachau and Belsen are dormant within us all.

And how, in the approved manner, might I have effected these ends? Dramatically, perhaps. A confrontation with the deranged Headmaster, the mirrored sunglasses worn even in his dim room, the venetian blinds permanently shuttered.

David and Goliath.

Or, more obliquely, affectingly, by an encounter at a later date with the recaptured Dennis.

Simple enough to do.

But I can't be bothered.

It was while I was writing this story that something happened which disturbed me, which made the task of writing not only tedious but offensive.

What happened was this.

It was Open Evening at the public school my son and daughter attend. My wife and I dutifully turned out, watched the entertainment provided, the thumping gymnastics, the incomprehensible play written and performed by the kids in Grade Seven, renditions by the choir, two trios, a quartet, and the ukulele ensemble. We then inspected our children's grubby exercise books which we see every day anyway, admired the

Easter decorations, cardboard rabbit-shapes with glued-on absorbent-cotton tails etc. Smiled and chatted to their teachers. A necessary evening of unrelieved dreariness.

And driving back home along the dark country roads replying to my children's back-seat interrogation—Which did you like best? The gymnastics? The choir? What about the play? Wasn't the play funny?—and assuring my wife that I wasn't driving too fast, that the road wasn't icy, I passed the township dump. The dump was on fire. I looked down on the scene for only a few seconds. Twisting above the red heart of the fire, yellow tongues of flame. In the light thrown by the flames, grey smoke piling up to merge with the darkness of the night. Two figures. And high in the night sky, a few singing sparks. Then the sight was gone.

At that moment, my heart filled with a kind of—it's a strange word to use, perhaps, almost embarrassing, but I *will* say it—filled with a kind of *joy.*

What disturbed me, upset me, was that the feeling was so violent, so total. No. No, that's not what upset me. In the aftermath of that feeling, what upset me was its *strangeness*, the realization that I'd felt nothing like it for so many years.

Since then, and during the time I've been trying to finish up this story, I've been thinking about Dennis, for there *was* a Dennis, though I have no idea now what his name was. Let's call him Dennis and be done with it. Those events, in so far as they're at all autobiographical, happened more than twenty years ago in a country which is foreign to me now. So. Dennis. I've been thinking about him. And me.

And the vision of fire at night.

Fire at night seen through winter trees.

Drifting into sleep or lying half-awake, I picture fire. And I'm filled with an envious longing. Though I ought to qualify 'envious'. As I qualify most things. This isn't making much sense, is it? But listen. This is difficult for me, too. I want to make clear, you see, that I'm in no way romanticizing Dennis. I think that's important.

I know his life quite intimately. Much to my parents' distress, I admired his local counterparts and played with them for much of my childhood. I can imagine the pacifier smeared with Tate and Lyle's Golden Syrup when he was a baby, the late and irregular hours as an infant. On the casually wiped oilcloth of the kitchen table, the buns with sticky white icing and the cluster of pop bottles. I can imagine him and his brother and sister like a litter of hot-bellied puppies squabbling, gorging, sleeping where they dropped oblivious to the constant blare of the TV and radio. I can see his sister, off to school in a party frock, his snot-blocked brother with the permanent stye. And as Dennis grew a little older, ragtag games that surged in the surrounding streets till long past dusk.

I know his mother, warm and generous but too busy and always too tired. Too soft with him, too, after his father died. Not a stupid woman but slow and easy-going. I can see her dressing herself up on Friday nights in a parody of her youth, a few too many at the local, and after the death of her husband, consoling herself with a succession of uncles who'd give Dennis a couple of bob to go to the pictures to get him out of the way.

And then the drift into playing where one should not play, railway-yards perhaps, bouncing on the lumber in timber-yards, the pleasures of being chased. And as the world of school closed against him—hand-me-downs, incomprehension, hot tears in the school lavatories—the more aggressive acts. Street lights shot out, bricks through windows, feuds in the parks, and running stone-fights with rival gangs across the bomb-sites where willow herb still grew. Webley air-pistols, sheath knives, an accident involving stitches. Shoplifting in Woolworth's. Padlocks splintered from a shed. And edging towards the adult world, packets of Weights and Woodbines bought in fives, beer supplied by laughing older brothers, and, queasily, the girl up his street they all had, the girl from the special school.

And, years past the year I knew him, I can see him in the pub he's made his local, dressed to kill, his worldly wealth his wardrobe, dangerous with that bristling code of honour which demands satisfaction outside of those whose eyes dare more than glance...

No. I'm not romanticizing Dennis.

I wonder what became of him. Did he become a labourer perhaps? Carrying a hod 'on the buildings', as he'd say? Or is he one of an anonymous tide flowing in through factory gates? Difficult to imagine the Dennis I knew settling down to that kind of grind. More probably he's on unemployment or doing time for some bungled piece of breaking and entering.

Dennis.

I *did* see Dennis again after I'd left the Approved School that afternoon. I saw him after he'd been recaptured. I know I'm not organizing this very well. It's difficult for me to say what I want to say.

It happened like this. I'd got another job in Eastmill almost immediately in a Secondary Modern School. Dr. James—let's call him that anyway—got the information from my parents, whose address was on the application I'd filed at the Reception Centre. He phoned me at the school and told me that Dennis had been caught in London, had been held down naked over a table by Uncle Arthur and Mr. Austyn and savagely birched by our friend in the sunglasses, was in the Eastmill Sick Bay, was feverish, and kept on asking for me. Dr. James, with considerable bravery given his personality and circumstances, smuggled me in one evening to see the boy. He was obviously in pain, his face gaunt, the eyes big and shadowed, but he smiled to see me and undid his pyjama jacket carefully, slowly, lifting it aside to show me his chest. His brother, the one in the army who'd been home on leave, had paid for it. It was just possible to distinguish the outlines of a sailing ship through the crust of red and blue and green, the whole mess raised, heaving, cracking in furry scabs.

I can't remember what we said. I do remember the way he undid the jacket as though uncovering an icon and the tremendous heat his infected chest gave off.

This incident, now I come to think about it, would have made a suitable ending to the story. Touching. The suggestion of a kind of victory, however limited, over the forces of evil. David and Goliath. Readers like that sort of thing. But it would have been a sentimental lie.

Dennis was no hero. He was a bloody nuisance then and he's doubtless a bloody nuisance now. And the staff of that school weren't evil, though at one time, my mind clouded by the prating of A. S. Neil and such, I doubtless thought so. They were merely stupid. Their answer to the problem of Dennis was crude, but it was at least an answer. I just don't *know* any more. Time and experience seem to have stripped me of answers.

My life has been what most people would call 'successful'. I have a respected career. My opinions on this and that are occasionally sought. Sometimes I have been asked to address conventions. I love my wife. I love my children. I live a pleasant life in a pleasant house.

What, then, is the problem?

Fire at night seen through the forms of winter trees.

That is the problem.

You see, what I'm trying to get at, Dennis, is this. They told you all your life, the Wechsler-Bellevue merchants, the teachers, the guardians of culture, and, yes, me, I suppose, that you were wrong, stupid, headed for a bad end. But you had something, *knew* something they didn't. Something *I* didn't. Do you see now why it's so important for me to stress that I'm not romanticizing your life, Dennis, or the lives of the ignorant yobs and louts who were your friends? You can't even begin to grasp how appalling it is for me to attempt to say this. Say what? That my life, respectable, sober, industrious, and civilized, above all civilized, has at its core a desolating emptiness. That, quite simply, you in your stupid, feckless way have enjoyed life more than I have.

I've never escaped, you see, Dennis. I've never lived off hostile country.

Did you burn down houses in Penge? I don't know, can't remember if I invented that. But if you *did*, the blood gorging you with excitement, the smoke, the roar as the whole thing got a grip—I can hardly bring myself to say this, *must* say this—*if* you did, *Christ!* it must have been wonderful.

You don't understand, do you, what it means for me to make these confessions? To *have* to make these confessions, to face the death I feel inside myself?

Let me try to put this in a different way. Let me try to find words that perhaps you'll understand. Words! Understand! Good Christ, will it never end, this blathering!

Dennis. Dennis. Listen!

Dennis, I envy you your—

Christ, man! Out with it!

Dennis. Listen to me.

Concentrate.

Dennis, I wish *I* had a tattoo.

The Nipples of Venus

Rome stank of exhaust fumes and below our hotel room on the Via Sistina motor bikes and scooters snarled and ripped past late into the night rattling the window and the plywood wardrobe. The bathroom, a boxed-in corner, was the size of two upright coffins. It was impossible to sit on the toilet without jamming your knees against the wash-basin. In the chest of drawers, Helen discovered crackers, crumbs, and Pan Am cheese.

I'd reserved the room by phone from Florence, choosing the hotel from a guidebook from a list headed: Moderate. We would only have to put up with it for Saturday and Sunday and would then fly home on Monday. After nearly three weeks spent mainly in Florence and Venice, I had no real interest in looking at things Roman. I felt...not tired, exactly. Couldn't take in any more. I'd had enough. 'Surfeited' was the word, perhaps. I was sick of cameras and photographs and tourists and tourism and disliking myself for being part of the problem. I felt burdened by history, ashamed of my ignorance, numbed by the succession of *ponte*, *porta*, *piazza*, and *palazzo*. I was beginning to feel like...who was it? Twain, I think, Mark Twain, who when asked what he'd thought of Rome said to his wife:

Was that the place we saw the yellow dog?

Helen was bulged and bloated and the elastic of her underpants and pantyhose had left red weals and ribbing on the flesh of her stomach. She'd been constipated for nearly two weeks.

I'd told her to stop eating pasta, to relax, to stop worrying about whether the children would leave the iron switched on, about aviation disasters, devaluation of the lira, cancer of the colon, but at night I heard her sighing, grinding her teeth, restless under the sheets, gnawing on the bones of her worries.

That waiter in—where was it? Milan? No. Definitely not in Milan. Bologna?—a waiter who'd worked for some years in Soho in the family restaurant—he'd told us that the tortellini, the tiny stuffed shells of pasta in our soup, were commonly called 'the nipples of Venus'.

Fettuccine, tuffolini, capelletti, manicotti, gnocchi...

Mia moglie è malata.

Dov'è una farmacia?

Aspirina?

Bicarbonato di soda?

...polenta, rigatoni, tortellini...

Praaaaaaaaap...

Scooters on the Via Sistina.

Praaaaaaaaap...

Helen passing gas.

T he Spanish Steps were just at the top of the street anyway and at the very least, Helen said, we had to see the Trevi Fountain and St. Peter's and the Pantheon.

They all looked much as they looked in photographs. Not as attractive, really. The Spanish Steps were littered with American college students. The sweep of St. Peter's Square was ruined even at that early hour by parked coaches from Luton, Belgrade, Brussels, and Brighton. Knowing that St. Peter's itself would be hung with acres of martyrdom and suchlike, I refused to set foot in it. The Trevi Fountain was rimmed with people taking its photograph and was magnificent but disappointing.

Places of historical interest often make me feel as if I'm eight again and the sermon will never end. I enjoyed the *doors* of the Pantheon—I always seem drawn to bronze—but the hushed interior struck me as lugubrious. Helen, on the other hand, is an inveterate reader of every notice, explication, plaque, and advisement.

Straightening up and taking off her reading glasses, she says,

"This is the tomb of Raphael."

"How about a coffee?"

"Born 1483."

"Espresso. You like that. In the square."

"Died in 1520."

"Nice coffee."

And then it was back to the Spanish Steps because she wanted to go jostling up and down the Via Condotti looking in the windows—Ferragamo, Gabrielli, Bulgari, Valentino, Gucci. And then in search of even more pairs of shoes, purses, scarves, gloves, and sweaters, it was down to the stores and boutiques on the Via del Tritone.

For lunch I ate *funghi arrosto alla Romana*. Helen ordered *risotto alla parmigiana* and had to go back to the hotel. She said she'd just lie there for a bit and if the pains went away she'd have a little nap. She asked me if I thought it was cancer, so I said that people with cancer *lost* weight and that it was *risotto, manifestly* risotto, *risotto first and last.*

"There's no need to shout at me."

"I am *not* shouting. I am speaking emphatically."

"You don't mind?" she said. "Really?"

"I'll go for a stroll around," I said.

"You won't feel I'm deserting you?"

"Just rest."

I strolled up the Via Sistina and stood looking down the sweep of the Spanish Steps. Then sauntered on. Some seventy-five yards to the right of the Steps, seventy-five yards or so past the Trinità dei Monti along the stretch of gravel road which leads into the grounds of the Villa Borghese, tucked away behind a thick hedge and shaded by trees, was an outdoor café hidden in a narrow garden. The garden was just a strip between the road and the edge of the steep hill which fell away down towards the Via Condotti or whatever was beneath. The Piazza di Spagna, perhaps. Houses must have been built almost flush with the face of the hill because through the screening pampas grass I could glimpse below the leaning rusty fence at the garden's edge the warm ripple of terra cotta roof tiles.

The garden was paved with stone flagstones. Shrubs and flowers grew in low-walled beds and urns. In the centre of the garden was a small rectangular pond with reeds growing in it, the flash of fish red and gold. The tall hedge which hid the garden from the road was dark, evergreen, yew trees.

It was quiet there, the traffic noises muted to a murmur. Round white metal tables shaded by gay umbrellas, white folding chairs. Two old waiters were bringing food and drinks from the hut at the garden's entrance. There were only three couples and a family at the tables. The yew hedge was straggly and needed cutting back. The shrubs and flowers in the stone-walled beds were gone a little to seed, unweeded.

I sat at the only table without an umbrella, a table set into a corner formed by the hedge and a low stone wall. The wall screened the inner garden a little from the openness of the entrance and from the shingled hut-like place the food came from. All along the top of the wall stood pots of geraniums and jutting out from the wall near my corner table was the basin of a fountain. The basin was in the form of a scallop shell. The stone shell looked much older than the wall. It looked as if it had come down in the world, ending up here in this garden café after gracing for two hundred years or more some ducal garden or palazzo courtyard. The stone was softer than the stone of the wall, grainy, the sharpness of its cuts and flutes blurred and weathered.

I sat enjoying the warmth of the sun. The Becks beer bottle and my glass were beaded with condensation. Sparrows were hopping between tables pecking crumbs. Water was trickling down the wall and falling into the stone scallop shell from a narrow copper pipe which led away down behind the wall and towards the hut at the garden's entrance. Where the pipe crossed the central path feet had squashed it almost flat. The small sound of the water was starting to take over my mind. The glint and sparkle of the sunlight on the water, the tinkling sound of it, the changes in the sound of it as it rose and deepened around the domed bronze grate before draining—it all held me in deepening relaxation.

Somewhere just below me were famous guidebook attractions—the Barcaccia Fountain, the Antico Caffe Greco, the rooms where John Keats died now preserved as a museum and containing memorabilia of Byron and Shelley—but all I wanted of Rome was to sit on in the sunshine drinking cold beer and listening to the loveliness of water running, the trill and spirtle, the rill and trickle of it.

Watching the sparrow, the small cockings of its head, watching the little boy in the white shirt and red bow-tie balancing face-down over his father's thigh, I was aware suddenly at the corner of my eye of flickering movement. I turned my head and there, reared up on its front legs on the rim of the stone scallop shell, was a lizard. It stood motionless. I turned more towards it. Its back was a matte black but its throat and neck and sides were touched with a green so brilliant it looked almost metallic, as if it had been dusted with metallic powder.

Set on the stone surround of the scallop shell were two pots of geraniums and from the shadow of these now appeared another lizard, smaller than the first, not as dark in colouring, dun rather than black and with not a trace of the shimmering peacock green—compared with the male a scrawny creature drab and dowdy.

This lizard waddled down into the curve of the stone basin where she stopped and raised her head as if watching or listening. Or was she perhaps scenting what was on the air? I'd read somewhere that snakes 'smelled' with their tongues. Were lizards, I wondered, like snakes in that? Would they go into water? Was she going to drink?

I was startled by loud rustlings in the hedge near my chair. A bird? A bird rootling about in dead leaves. But it wasn't that kind of noise quite. Not as loud. And, I realized, it was more continuous than the noise a bird would have made—rustling, twig-snipping, pushing, scuffling. The noise was travelling along *inside* the hedge. Slowly, cautiously, not wanting to frighten away the lizards on the stone scallop shell, I bent and parted branches, peering.

And then the noise stopped.

As I sat up, I saw that the stone bowl was empty, the brown lizard disappeared behind the geranium pots again. The green lizard was still motionless where he'd been before. Every few seconds his neck pulsed. Suddenly I saw on the wall level with my knee a lizard climbing. Every two or three inches it stopped, clinging, seeming to listen. It too was green but it had no tail. Where its tail should have been was a glossy rounded stump.

Lacking the tail's long grace, the lizard looked unbalanced, clumsy. About half the tail was gone. It was broken off just below that place where the body tapered. The stump was a scaleless wound, shiny, slightly bulbous, in colour a very dark red mixed with black. The end of the stump bulged out like a blob of smoke-swirled sealing-wax.

Just as its head was sticking up over the edge of the stone shell, the other lizard ran at it. The mutilated lizard turned and flashed halfway down the wall but then stopped, head-down, clinging. The pursuing lizard stopped too and cocked its head at an angle as if hearing something commanding to its right.

Seconds later, the stubby lizard skittered down the rest of the wall, but then stopped again on the flagstones. The pursuing lizard pursued but himself stopped poised above the wall's last course of stones. It was like watching the flurry of a silent movie with the action frozen every few seconds. And then the damaged lizard was negotiating in dreamy slow motion dead twigs and blown leaves on his way back into the hedge. He *clambered* over them as if they were thick boughs, back legs cocked up at funny angles like a cartoon animal, crawling, ludicrous. His pursuer faced in the opposite direction intently, fiercely.

Peculiar little creatures.

I signalled to the waiter for another beer.

I sat on in the sunshine, drifting, smelling the smell on my fingers of crushed geranium leaves, listening to the sounds the water made.

And then the noises in the hedge started again.

And again the lizard with the stump was climbing the wall.

And again the lizard on the top was rushing at it, driving it down.

By the time I was finishing my third beer, the attacks and retreats were almost continuous. The stubby lizard always climbed the wall at exactly the same place. The defending lizard always returned to the exact spot on the stone surround of the scallop shell where the attacking lizard would appear. The stop-frame chases flowed and halted down the wall, across the flagstones, halted, round an urn, into the hedge.

But with each sortie the damaged lizard was being driven further and further away. Finally, the pursuing lizard hauled his length into the hedge and I listened to their blundering progress over the litter of twigs and rusty needles in the hedge-bottom, the rustlings and cracklings, the scrabblings travelling further and further away from my chair until there was silence.

The sun had moved around the crown of the tree and was now full on me. I could feel the sweat starting on my chest, in the hollow of my throat, the damp prickle of sweat in my groin. I glanced at my watch to see how long she'd been sleeping. I thought of strolling back to the hotel and having a shower, but the thought of showering in the boxed-in bathroom inside the glass device with its folding glass doors like a compressed telephone booth—the thought of touching with every movement cold, soap-slimy glass...

I lifted the empty Becks bottle and nodded at the waiter as he passed.

A dragon-fly hovered over the pond, its wings at certain angles a blue iridescence.

I wondered about my chances of finding a Roman restaurant or trattoria serving *Abbracchio alla Romana*, a dish I'd read about with interest. And while I was thinking about restaurants and roast lamb flavoured with rosemary and anchovies and about poor Helen's *risotto* and about how long I'd been sitting in the garden and Helen worrying there in that plywood room heavy with exhaust fumes...

you might have been killed ... you know I only nap for an hour ... I got so scared ...

...while I was thinking about this and these and listening to the water's trickle and looking at the white, heavy plumes of the pampas grass, there on top of the wall, my eye caught by the movement, was the lizard with the stump.

I studied the face of the wall, scanned the bottom of the hedge, looked as far around the base of the urn as I could see without moving, but there was no sign of the other lizard, no sound of pursuit.

He stood motionless on top of the wall just above the scallop shell where the scrawny brown female still basked. The stump looked as if blood and flesh had oozed from the wound and then hardened into this glossy, bulging scab.

The coast's clear, Charlie!

Come on!

Come on!

He was clinging head-down to the wall inches above the stone shell.

The female had raised her head.

Now he seemed to be studying a pale wedge of crumbling mortar.

Come on!

And then he waddled down onto the stone surround and seized the female lizard firmly about the middle in his jaws. They lay at right angles to each other as if catatonic. The female's front right leg dangled in the air.

Come on, you gimpy retard! Let go! You're biting the wrong one. It's the GREEN ones we bite. The brown ones are the ones we...

The waiter's voice startled me.

I smiled, shook my head, picked up the four cash-register slips, leaned over to one side to get at my wallet in my back pocket. When he'd gone and I turned back to the stone scallop shell, the female had already vanished and the end of the stump, somewhere between the colour of a ripening blackberry and a blood blister, was just disappearing into the shadows behind one of the pots of geraniums.

I got up slowly and quietly. I was careful not to scrape my chair on the flagstones. I set it down silently. I looked down to make sure my shoe wasn't going to knock against one of the table's tubular legs. One by one, I placed the coins on the saucer.

No, I told Helen on Sunday morning, not the Forum, not the Colosseum, not the Capitoline, the Palatine, or the Quirinal. I wanted to be lazy. I wanted to be taken somewhere. But not to monuments. Trees and fields. But not *walking*. I didn't want to *do* anything. I wanted to see farmhouses and outbuildings. What I wanted—yes, that was it exactly— a coach tour! I wanted to gaze out of the window at red and orange roof tiles, at ochre walls, poppies growing wild on the roadsides, vines.

At 10 a.m. we were waiting in a small office in a side street for the arrival of the coach. The brochure in the hotel lobby had described the outing as Extended Alban Hills Tours— Castelli Romani. Our coach was apparently now touring some of the larger hotels picking up other passengers. The whole operation seemed a bit makeshift and fly-by-night. The two young men running it seemed to do nothing but shout denials on the phone and hustle out into the street screaming at drivers as coach after coach checked in at the office before setting out to tour whatever they were advertised as touring. Commands and queries were hysterical. Tickets were counted and recounted. And then recounted. Coaches were finally dispatched with operatic gesture as if they were full of troops going up to some heroic Front.

As each coach pulled up, we looked inquiry at one or other of the young men. 'This is not yours,' said their hands. 'Patience.' 'Do not fear. When your conveyance arrives, we will inform you,' said their gestures.

We were both startled by the entry of a large, stout man with a shaved head who barged into the tiny office saying something that sounded challenging or jeering. His voice was harsh. He limped, throwing out one leg stiffly. Helen sat up in the plastic chair and drew her legs in. Something about his appearance suggested that he'd survived a bad car-crash. He leaned on an aluminum stick which ended in a large rubber bulb. He was wearing rimless blue-tinted glasses. His lip was permanently drawn up a little at one side. There was a lot of visible metal in his teeth. He stumped about in the confined space shouting and growling.

The young man with the mauve leather shoes shouted 'no' a lot and 'never' and slapped the counter with a plastic ruler. The other young man picked up a glossy brochure and, gazing fixedly at the ceiling, twisted it as if wringing a neck. The shaven-headed man pushed a pile of pamphlets off the counter with the rubber tip of his aluminum stick.

A coach pulled up and a young woman in a yellow dress got down from it and clattered on heels into the office. They all shouted at her. She spat—*teh*—and made a coarse gesture.

The young man with the mauve leather shoes went outside to shout up at the coach driver. Through the window, we watched him counting, pulling each finger down in turn.

...five, six, *seven*.

Further heart-rending pantomime followed.

Still in full flow, he burst back into the office brandishing the tickets in an accusatory way. Peering and pouting into the mirror of a compact, the girl in the yellow dress continued applying lipstick. They all shouted questions at her, possibly rhetorical. The horrible shaven-headed man shook the handle of his aluminum cane in her face.

She spat again—*teh*.

The bus driver sounded his horn.

The other young man spoke beseechingly to the potted azalea.

"Is that," said Helen, "the Castelli Romani coach? Or isn't it the Castelli Romani coach?"

There was silence as everyone stared at her.

"It *is*, dear madam, it *is*," said the horribly bald man.

"Good," said Helen.

And I followed her out.

We nodded to the other seven passengers as we climbed aboard and seated ourselves behind them near the front of the coach. They sounded American. There were two middle-aged couples, a middle-aged man on his own, rather melancholy-looking, and a middle-aged man with an old woman.

"Here he comes goosewalking," said Helen.

"*Stepping*," I said.

The shaven-headed man, leg lifting up and then swinging to the side, was stumping across the road leaning on the aluminum cane. His jacket was a flapping black-and-white plaid.

"Oh, *no*!" I said. "You don't think *he's*..."

"I told you," said Helen. "I told you this was going to be awful."

The shaven-headed man climbed up into the bus, hooked his aluminum cane over the handrail above the steps, and unclipped the microphone. Holding it in front of his mouth, he surveyed us.

"Today," he said with strange, metallic sibilance, "today you are my children."

Helen nudged.

"Today I am taking you into the Alban Hills. I will show you many wonders. I will show you extinct volcanoes. I will show you the lake of the famous Caligula. I will show you the headquarters of the German Army in World War II. Together we will visit Castel Gandolfo, Albano, Genzano, Frascati, and Rocca di Papa. We will leave ancient Rome by going past the Colosseum and out onto the Via Appia Antica completed by Appius Claudius in 312 before Christ."

He nodded slowly.

"Oh yes, my children."

Still nodding.

"*Before Christ.*"

He looked from face to face.

"You will know this famous road as the Appian Way and you will have seen it in the movie *Spartacus* with the star Kirk Douglas."

"Oh, God!" said Helen.

"Well, my children," he said, tapping the bus driver on the shoulder, "are you ready? But you are curious about me. Who *is* this man, you are saying."

He inclined his shaved head in a bow.

"*Who* am I?"

He chuckled into the microphone.

"They call me Kojak."

Cypresses standing guard along the Appian Way over sepulchres and sarcophagi, umbrella pines shading fragments of statuary. Tombs B.C. Tombs A.D. Statuary contemporaneous with Julius Caesar, of whom we would have read in the play of that name by William Shakespeare. It was impossible to ignore or block out his voice, and after a few minutes we'd come to dread the clicking on of the microphone and the harsh, metallic commentary.

You will pay attention to your left and you will see...

A sarcophagus.

You will pay attention opposite and you will see...

"Opposite what?"

"He means straight ahead."

"Oh."

...to your right and in one minute you will see a famous school for women drivers...

Into view hove a scrap-metal dealer's yard mountainous with wrecked cars.

You will pay attention...

But despite the irritation of the rasping voice, I found the expedition soothing and the motion of the coach restful. The landscape as it passed was pleasing. Fields. Hedges. Garden plots. The warmth of terra cotta tiles. Hills. White clouds in a sky of blue.

The Pope's summer residence at Castel Gandolfo was a glimpse through open ornate gates up a drive to a house, then the high encircling stone wall around the park.

Beech trees.

In the narrow, steep streets of the small town, the coach's length negotiated the sharp turns, eased around corners, trundled past the elaborate façade of the church and through the piazza with its fountain by Bernini.

The famous Peach Festival took place in June.

At Lake Albano we were to stop for half an hour.

No less, my children, and no more.

The coach pulled into the restaurant parking lot and backed into line with more than a dozen others. The restaurant, a cafeteria sort of place, was built on the very edge of the lake. It was jammed with tourists. Washrooms were at the bottom of a central staircase and children ran up and down the stairs, shouting. There was a faint smell of disinfectant. Lost children cried.

In the plastic display cases were sandwiches with dubious fillings, tired-looking panini, and slices of soggy pizza that were being reheated in microwave ovens until greasy.

The man from our coach who was travelling with the old woman sat staring out of the plate-glass window which overlooked the lake. The old woman was spooning in with trembling speed what looked like a huge English trifle, mounds of whipped cream, maraschino cherries, custard, cake.

Helen and I bought an ice cream we didn't really want. We stood on the wooden dock beside the restaurant and looked at the lake which was unnaturally blue. There was a strong breeze. White sails were swooping over the water. I felt cold and wished we could get back in the coach.

"So this was a volcano," said Helen.

"I guess so."

"The top blew off and then it filled up with water."

"I suppose that's it."

The man from our coach who was on his own, the melancholy-looking man, wandered onto the other side of the dock. He stood holding an ice-cream cone and looking across the lake. He looked a bit like Stan Laurel. We nodded to him. He nodded to us and made a sort of gesture at the lake with his ice cream as if to convey approval.

We smiled and nodded.

The engine of the coach was throbbing as we sat waiting for the man and the old woman to shuffle across the parking lot. The stiff breeze suddenly blew the man's hair down, revealing him as bald. From one side of his head hung a long hank which had been trained up and over his bald pate. He looked naked and bizarre as he stood there, the length of hair hanging from the side of his head and fluttering below his shoulder. It looked as if he'd been scalped. The attached hair looked like a dead thing, like a pelt.

Seemingly unembarrassed, he lifted the hair back, settling it as if it were a beret, patting it into place. The old woman stood perhaps two feet from the side of the coach smiling at it with a little smile.

And so, my children, we head now for Genzano and for Frascati, the Queen of the Castelli...

We did not stop in Genzano which also had Baroque fountains possibly by Bernini in the piazzas and a palazzo of some sort. Down below the town was the Lake of Nemi from which two of Caligula's warships had been recovered only to be burned by the retreating Adolf Hitler.

The famous Feast of Flowers took place in May.

"Why do I know the name Frascati?" said Helen.

"Because of the wine?"

"Have I had it?"

I shrugged.

"I had some *years* ago," I said. "Must be thirty years ago now—at a wedding. We drank it with strawberries."

"Whose wedding?"

"And I don't think I've had it since. Um? Oh...a friend from college. I haven't heard from him—Tony Cranbrook...oh, it's been *years*."

"There," said Helen, "what kind of tree is that?"

I shook my head.

Frascati.

The wine was dry and golden.

Gold in candlelight.

The marriage of Tony Cranbrook had been celebrated in the village church, frayed purple hassocks, that special Anglican smell of damp and dust and stone, marble memorials let into the wall:

...departed this life June 11th 1795 in the sure and certain hope of the resurrection and of the life everlasting...

Afterwards, the younger people had strolled back through deep lanes to the family house for the reception. I'd walked with a girl called Susan who turned out to be the sister of one of the bridesmaids. She'd picked a buttercup and lodged it behind her ear. She'd said:

Do you know what this means in Tahiti?

Late in the evening they'd been wandering about the house calling to us to come and eat strawberries, calling out that I had to make another speech.

Jack?

We know you're there!

Susan?

Jack and Su-san!

The larger drawing-room was warm and quick with candle-light. In the centre of the dark polished refectory table stood a gleaming silver épergne piled with tiny wild strawberries. By the side of it stood octagonal silver sugar casters. The candelabra on the table glossed the wood's dark grain. Reflected in the épergne's curves and facets, points of flame quivered.

You will pay attention to your right...

Traffic was thickening.

Fisher!

The bus was slowing.

Susan Fisher!

...above the piazza. The Villa is still owned by the Aldobrandini family. You will notice the central avenue of box trees. The park is noted for its grottos and Baroque fountains.

"Doubtless by Bernini," I said.

"Is that a *palm* tree?" said Helen.

The Villa is open to tourists only in the morning and upon application to the officials of the Frascati Tourist Office. If you will consult your watches, you will see that it is now afternoon so we will proceed immediately to the largest of the Frascati wine cellars.

The aluminum cane with its rubber bulb thumping down, the leg swinging up and to the side, Kojak led the straggling procession towards a large grey stone building at the bottom end of the sloping piazza. A steep flight of steps led down to a terrace and the main entrance. Kojak, teeth bared with the exertion, started to stump and crab his way down.

"Oh, look at the poor old thing, Jack," said Helen. "He'll never manage her on his own down here."

I went back across the road to where they were still waiting to cross and put my arm under the old woman's. She seemed almost weightless.

"I appreciate this," he said, nodding vigorously on the other side of her. "Nelson Morrison. We're from Trenton, New Jersey."

"Not at all," I said. "Not at all. It's a pleasure."

The old woman did not look at either of us.

"That's the way," I said. "That's it."

"She's not a big talker. She doesn't speak very often, do you, Mother?"

Step by step we edged her down.

"But she enjoys it, don't you, Mother? You can tell she enjoys it. She likes to go out. We went on a boat, didn't we, Mother?"

"Nearly there," I said.

"Do you remember the boat in Venice, Mother? Do you? I think it's a naughty day today, isn't it? You're only hearing what you want to hear."

"One more," I said.

"But she did enjoy it. Every year you'll find us somewhere, won't he, Mother?"

Inside, the others were sitting at a refectory table in a vaulted cellar. It was lit by bare bulbs. It was cool, almost cold, after coming in out of the sunshine. In places, the brickwork glistened with moisture. Kojak, a cigarette held up between thumb and forefinger, was holding forth.

The cellars apparently extended under the building for more than a mile of natural caves and caverns. In the tunnels and corridors were more than a million bottles of wine. Today, however, there was nothing to see as the wine-making did not take place until September. But famous and authentic food was available at the café and counter just a bit further down the tunnel and bottles of the finest Frascati were advantageously for sale. If we desired to buy wine, it would be his pleasure to negotiate for us.

He paused.

He surveyed us through the blue-tinted spectacles.

Slowly, he shook his head.

The five bottles of wine on the table were provided free of

charge for us to drink on its own or as an accompaniment to food we might purchase. While he was talking, a girl with a sacking apron round her waist and with broken-backed men's shoes on her feet scuffed in with a tray of tumblers. Kojak started pouring the wine. It looked as if it had been drawn from a barrel minutes before. It was greenish and cloudy. It was thin and vile and tasted like tin. I decided to drink it quickly.

I didn't actually see it happen because I was leaning over saying something to Helen. I heard the melancholy man, the man who was travelling alone, say, "No thank you. I don't drink."

Glass chinking against glass.

"No thank you."

A chair scraping.

And there was Kojak mopping at his trouser leg with a handkerchief and grinding out what sounded like imprecations which were getting louder and louder. The melancholy man had somehow moved his glass away while Kojak was pouring or had tried to cover it or pushed away the neck of the bottle. Raised fist quivering, Kojak was addressing the vaulted roof.

Grabbing a bottle-neck in his meaty hand, he upended the bottle over the little man's glass, wine glugging and splashing onto the table.

"Doesn't drink!" snarled Kojak.

He slammed the bottle down on the table.

"Doesn't drink!"

He flicked drops of wine onto the table off the back of his splashed hand.

"Mama mia! Doesn't drink!"

Grinding and growling he stumped off towards the café.

He left behind him a silence.

Into the silence, one of the women said,

"Perhaps it's a custom you're supposed to drink it? If you don't it's insulting?"

"Now wait a minute," said her husband.

"Like covering your head?" she added.

"Maybe I'm out of line," said the other man, "but in my book that was inappropriate behaviour."

"I never did much like the taste of alcohol," said the melancholy man.

His accent was British and glumly northern.

"They seem to sup it with everything here," he said, shaking his head in gloomy disapproval.

"Where are you folks from?" said the man in the turquoise shirt.

"Canada," said Helen.

"You hear that, June? Ottawa? Did we visit Ottawa, June?"

"Maybe," said June, "being that he's European and..."

"It's nothing to do with being European," said Helen. "It's to do with being rude and a bully. And he's not getting a tip from *us*."

"Yeah," said June's husband, "and what's with all these jokes about women drivers? I'll tell you something, okay? *My wife drives better than I drive.* Okay?"

He looked around the table.

"Okay?"

"I've seen them," said the melancholy man, "in those little places where they eat their breakfasts standing up, I've seen them in there first thing in the morning—imagine—taking raw spirits."

The old woman sat hunched within a tweed coat, little eyes watching. She made me think of a fledgling that had fallen from the nest. Her tumbler was empty. She was looking at me. Then she seemed to be looking at the nearest bottle. I raised my eyebrows. Her eyes seemed to grow wider. I poured her more and her hand crept out to secure the glass.

"*Jack!*" whispered Helen.

"What the hell difference does it make?"

I poured more of the stuff for myself.

June and Chuck were from North Dakota. Norm and Joanne were from California. Chuck was in construction.

Norm was on a disability pension and sold patio furniture. Joanne was a nurse. George Robinson was from Bradford and did something to do with textile machinery. Nelson and his mother travelled every summer and last summer had visited Yugoslavia but had suffered from the food.

I explained to June that it was quite possible that I sounded very like the guy on a PBS series because the series had been made by the BBC and I had been born in the UK but was now Canadian. She told me my accent was cute. I told her I thought her accent cute too. We toasted each other's accents. Helen began giving me looks.

June had bought a purse in Rome. Joanne had bought a purse in Florence. Florence was noted for purses. June and Chuck were going to Florence after Rome. Helen had bought a purse in Florence—the best area of Florence for purses being on the far side of the Ponte Vecchio. In Venice there were far fewer stores selling purses. Shoes, on the other hand, shoe stores were everywhere. Norm said he'd observed more shoe stores in Italy than in any other country in the world.

Nelson disliked olive oil.

George could not abide eggplants. Doris, George's wife who had died of cancer the year before, had never fancied tomatoes.

Nelson was flushed and becoming loquacious.

Chuck said he'd had better pizza in Grand Forks, North Dakota, where at least they put cheese on it and it wasn't runny.

George said the look of eggplants made him think of native women.

Joanne said a little pasta went a long way.

Milan?

After Venice, Norm and Joanne were booked into Milan. What was Milan like? Had anyone been there?

"Don't speak to me about Milan!" said Helen.

"Not a favourite subject with us," I said.

"We got mugged there," said Helen, "and they stole a gold bracelet I'd had since I was twenty-one."

"'They'," I said, "being three girls."

"We were walking along on the sidewalk just outside that monstrous railway station..."

"Three *girls*, for Christ's sake!"

"They came running up to us," said Helen.

"Two of them not more than thirteen years old," I said, "and the other about eighteen or nineteen."

"One of them had a newspaper sort of folded to show columns of figures and another had a bundle of tickets of some sort and they were waving these in our faces..."

"And talking at us very loudly and quickly..."

"...and, well, *brandishing* these..."

"...and sort of grabbing at you, pulling your sleeve..."

"*Touching* you," said Helen.

"*Right!*" said Norm. "Okay."

"*Exactly*," said Joanne. "That's *exactly*..."

"And then," I said, "I felt the tallest girl's hand going inside my jacket—you know—to your inside pocket..."

"We were so *distracted*, you see," said Helen, "what with all the talking and them pointing at the paper and waving things under your nose and being *touched*..."

"So anyway," I said, "when I felt *that* I realized what was happening and I hit this girl's arm away and..."

"Oh, it was *awful!*" said Helen. "Because *I* thought they were just beggars, you see, or kids trying to sell lottery tickets or something, and I was really horrible to Jack for hitting this girl...I mean, he hit her *really hard* and I thought they were just begging so I couldn't believe he'd..."

"But the best part," I said, "was that I probably wasn't the main target in the first place because we walked on into the station and we were buying tickets—we were in the line— and Helen..."

"I'd suddenly felt the weight," said Helen. "The difference, I mean, and I looked down at my wrist and the bracelet was gone. I hadn't felt a thing when they'd grabbed it. Not with all that other touching. They must have pulled and broken the safety chain and..."

"Of course," I said, "I ran back to the entrance but..."

I spread my hands.

"Long gone."

"With us," said Joanne, "it was postcards and guidebooks they were waving about."

"Where?"

"Here. In Rome."

"Girls? The same?"

"Gypsies," said Norm.

"Did they get anything?" said Helen.

"A Leica," said Joanne.

"Misdirection of attention," said Norm.

"Were they girl-gypsies?" I said.

"Misdirecting," said Norm. "It's the basic principle of illusionism."

"I was robbed right at the airport," said Nelson.

"It must be a national *industry*," said George.

"They had a baby in a shawl and I was just standing there with Mother and they pushed this baby against my chest and well, naturally, you..."

"I don't *believe* this!" said Norm. "This I do not *believe*!"

"And while I was holding it, the other two women were shouting at me in Italian and they had a magazine they were showing me..."

"What did they steal?"

"Airplane ticket. Passport. Traveller's cheques. But I had some American bills in the top pocket of my blazer so they didn't get that."

"Did you feel it?" said Joanne.

He shook his head.

"No. They just took the baby and walked away and I only realized when I was going to change a traveller's cheque at the cambio office because we were going to get on the bus, weren't we, Mother?"

"A baby!" said June.

"But a few minutes later," said Nelson, "one of the women came up to me on her own with the ticket and my passport."

"Why would she give them back?" said Helen. "Don't they sell them to spies or something?"

"I paid her for them," said Nelson.

"Paid her?" said June.

"*Paid her!*" said Norm.

"*PAID!*" said Chuck.

"Ten dollars," said Nelson.

"They must have seen you coming!" said George.

"They must have seen *all* of you coming," said Chuck.

Nelson poured himself another murky tumbler of Frascati.

"It wasn't much," he said. "Ten dollars. She got what she wanted. I got what I wanted."

He shrugged. Raising the glass, he said,

"A short life but a merry one!"

We stared at him.

"I got what I wanted, didn't I, Mother? And then we went on the green and red bus, didn't we? Do you remember? On the green and red bus?"

The old woman started making loud squeak noises in her throat.

It was the first sound we'd heard her make.

She sounded like a guinea pig.

"It's time for tinkles!" sang Nelson. "It's tinkle time."

And raising her up and half carrying her to the door of the women's malodorous toilet, he turned with her, almost as if waltzing, and backed his way in.

*

...not entirely without incident.

Don't mention Milan to us!

...except for Helen's getting mugged.

It all made quite a good story, a story with which we regaled our friends and neighbours. We became quite practised in the telling of it. We told it at parties and over dinners, feeding each other lines.

But the story we told was a story different in one particular from what really happened—though Helen doesn't know that.

The scene often comes to mind. I see it when the pages blur. I see it in my desk-top in the wood's repetitive grain. I see it when I gaze unseeing out of the window of the restaurant after lunch, the sun hot on my shoulder and sleeve. I see it when I'm lying in bed in the morning in those drowsy minutes after being awakened by the clink and chink of Helen's bottles as she applies moisturizing cream, foundation, blush, and shadow.

Chuck from Grand Forks, North Dakota, had been right. They *had* seen all of us coming. Easy pickings. Meek and nearing middle age, ready to be fleeced, lambs to the slaughter.

She'd been the first female I'd hit since childhood. I hadn't intended to hit her hard. I'd moved instinctively. Her eyes had widened with the pain of it.

I'd noticed her even before she'd run towards us. Good legs, high breasts pushing at the tight grey cotton dress, long light-brown hair. She was wearing bright yellow plastic sandals. She had no make-up on and looked a bit grubby, looked the young gamin she probably was.

I'd been carrying a suitcase and felt sweaty even though it was early in the morning. Her hand as it touched the side of my chest, my breast, was cool against my heat.

When I struck her arm, there was no panic in her eyes, just a widening. There was a hauteur in her expression. Our eyes held each other's for what seemed long seconds.

When Helen discovered her bracelet gone, I hurried out of the vast ticket hall but under the colonnade and out of sight I slowed to a walk. There is no rational, sensible explanation for what followed.

I stood in the archway of the entrance. The two small girls had gone. She stood facing me across the width of the curving road. It was as if she'd been waiting for me.

We stood staring at each other.

Behind her was a sidewalk café. The white metal chairs and tables were screened by square white tubs containing small, bushy bay trees. The bays were dark and glossy. Dozens of sparrows hopped about on the edges of the tubs. Pigeons were pecking along the sidewalk near her feet. Among them was a reddish-brown pigeon and two white ones. In the strong morning light I could see the lines of her body under the grey cotton dress. She was gently rubbing at her arm.

Sitting there in Reardon's restaurant, drowsy in the sunshine after eating the Businessman's Luncheon Special ($4.95), the cream of celery soup, the minced-beef pie with ginger-coloured gravy, the french fries, the sliced string beans, waiting for the waitress to bring coffee, sitting there with the winter sun warm through the window on my shoulder and sleeve, I walk out of the shadow of the arch and stand waiting on the edge of the sidewalk. She nods to me. It is a nod which is casually intimate, a nod of acknowledgement and greeting. I wait for a gap in the sweeping traffic.

She watches me approaching.

Travelling Northward

Drawers stuck or shot their contents onto the floor; shirts refused to come out of their intricate plastic bags causing him to hurt himself on the hook on the back of the bathroom door; she had *again* hidden his beige writing trousers; *both* towels were soggy; the other armhole of his shirt eluded him; following her sluttish ablutions, the capless toothpaste had hardened so that he ended up with a *lump* in his mouth, a lump of the most horrid texture, a *deliberate* lump.

Every morning of his life, Robert Forde awoke in a state of intense and mounting irritation. He felt, every morning, as if nerve endings all over his body were exposed and that the world was brushing against him. For an hour or more after awakening, he blundered about the confines of the house gripped in elaborate rage.

The only things that to any extent calmed him were breakfast and reading matter: the newspaper, the mail, Canadian Tire catalogues.

In the morning, Robert Forde's body required coffee. It required it filtered rather than percolated and seemed to prefer a blend called Medaglia D'Oro. It required it scalding and it required it promptly. To deny it immediate coffee was to imperil his morning's work. His body he believed to be a kind of corporal ark which housed his ability to write; this ability was a thing mysterious, so fickle, so fragile, so frangible that it had to be borne with exquisite care. Such necessary care and

cosseting were not only his responsibility but the responsibility of those around him. These needs of his body in its
function as ark, as he had often explained to his wife, Sheila,
were nothing whatever to do with him in any *personal* sense.

Sheila understood all this imperfectly.

Her slowness in the kitchen, behaviour which he could not
consider anything but deliberate, drove him to the edge of
mad shouting. She always reheated the coffee with the gas at a
barely visible blue flicker, a proceeding which to his quivering
nerves seemed like an extended refinement of Chinese water
torture. His response to this provocation was to wrench the
flame to full roar. She, in turn, lowered it to invisibility again
niggling—*explosions, implosions, burns*—nattering—*fracturing,
shattering, shards.*

He had implored her—had thrust into her hands crumpled
bills—to buy a vessel which *could* withstand direct heat. Buy,
he had beseeched her, a fucking great *cast bloody iron pot*, but
she had worn him down with a drizzle of pissy and querulous
complaint about having to clean ferrous or enamel containers
with steel wool whereas with glass...

Was there, he had demanded, no such thing as *thick* glass?
Or glass specifically designed to withstand direct heat? Did her
memory stretch as far back as school test-tubes? What did she
imagine *retorts* were made of? He could scarcely believe that in
an age of such vaunted technological achievement the invention and manufacture of a simple glass coffee-pot was beyond
the capabilities of the industrialized world. Indeed, now that
he thought about it, he *knew* there were such pots. He could
clearly remember having seen them in the houses of other
people. He was forced to believe that she simply *did not want* a
normal coffee-pot, that she *wilfully*...

Had he not read in the paper the warnings about Corn-
ing Ware?

Would she mind repeating that? Had he not *what*? Had he
heard aright? Of *course* he hadn't read warnings in the
newspaper. What an *insensitive* question! He hadn't TIME to

read fucking warnings. His life was hemmed and harried by deadlines and pressures indescribable. *Some* people doubtless had time to read Corning-fucking-Ware-warnings but *he* wasn't one of them. All he wanted—and Christ! *was it much to ask?*—was a cup of coffee WHEN HE WANTED IT.

He was aware that his behaviour was, by normal standards, indefensible. The intensity of his morning rage frightened even him. Even as he glared at his cowed offspring who leapt to turn off the radio and who communicated with each other in dumb show, he was not entirely free of guilt. He was aware that most wives who retailed the day's meteorological forecast were not rewarded with shouted and intemperate abuse; he was aware that most fathers at weekends did not eat breakfast wearing industrial ear-mufflers, but as he had often explained to Sheila—and firmly believed—he was but a vehicle, a mere conduit, the hapless servant of a mistress wanton and capricious.

He had explained to Sheila—and firmly believed—that human contact in the morning made it that much more impossible to face the waiting page. Drivel concerning the likelihood of fog or freezing rain, requests to run quotidian errands, the discussion of bills, squabbling children, chatter, *noise*—all this dispersed his concentration, muddied what had welled up in the night, breached the *containment* necessary for his work. There was nothing, he had assured her, in any way *personal* in this; it was just that he did not wish to speak to her and did not wish her to speak to him.

It was his habit to stay in bed until his sons had left for school and Sheila had left for work but on this morning, sleep stirred by words, he had woken early.

He poked about in the jar of marmalade with the tip of his knife trying to capture chunks of peel while keeping the latest issue of *Capital Review* open with his elbow. The unstable pile of mail beneath the magazine dolloped onto the kitchen floor causing his forefinger to marmalade itself. Slowly, and with such massive self-control that his temples throbbed, he wiped his finger on his place-mat.

Sheila did not look up; her fingers crept out from behind the newspaper for more of the whitish, pungent cheese and olives, a breakfast he considered Levantine and faintly disgusting.

The magazine did not review his last book. Did review seven chapbooks of unspeakable verse mainly by disgruntled females; did review, sycophantically, Grossman's latest assault on the English language; did review—his eye shied from the word 'epistemological'—the halitosis man.

He dropped it on his discard pile; to which he also added a request to review, a questionnaire from a sociology student at York University who was writing a paper on the income of Canadian writers, and an invitation to make a submission before a commission on the role of the arts in society in Ontario.

"Role of my rectum!"

"Pardon?"

"My orifice in Ontario!"

"What is it?"

"Rubbish. Nothing. This coffee's too strong again."

"Not for me it isn't."

He glanced up at her.

She continued reading the paper.

He stared for a moment at the crown of her bowed head, stared at the startling blaze of hair like a small star almost white at which she glanced in every mirror. Radiating from this central blaze, grey threads glistening in the black sheen.

Yet another thick manila envelope. He knew what it would contain. He sighed and tossed it onto the counter to open and read later in the day.

It would contain a manuscript by a young writer who realized how busy he was but dared to hope that he wouldn't mind just jotting down several pages of single-spaced constructive criticism of the enclosed which had been written under considerable personal difficulties.

"What's that?" said Sheila.

"What is what?" he said, keeping his eyes on the letter he

was inserting into the holder he had constructed from two wire coat-hangers and which sat between them on the breakfast table.

"That."

"This?"

He studied her over the rim of his cup, daring her to go on.

"Just a letter."

"I can see that," said Sheila. "Who's it from?"

"It's from some people in North Portage."

"Where's that?"

He sighed.

"I have no idea where North Portage is. The address claims it to be in Ontario. Judging from the sound of it, possibly somewhere to the north."

"What people?"

He pretended to consult the letter.

"The North Portage Thursday Evening."

"What do they want?"

"They want me to go there and do a reading and so forth."

"You're not going?"

He shrugged.

Sipping his coffee, he studied the letter.

The readings took place in a conducive space above Berman's Dry Goods and Winter Storage. Accommodation was a problem. The hotel was more a tavern and its rates, though low, were beyond the means of the Thursday Evening. He was welcome to stay with the undersigned. Or he could stay at the apartment of an Evening member and the person with whom he lived as they would be away on vacation. It was hoped that he enjoyed good home cooking.

He sat thinking about this.

He was strongly opposed to staying with the undersigned whose name, improbably, looked like 'Martin Prunes'. He had always considered the words 'good home cooking' ominous. 'The person with whom he lives'—he wondered what irregularity *that* implied. But the vacated apartment sounded promising; it was always a pleasure to snoop about in other people's houses.

For some odd reason, he also liked the sound of Berman's Dry Goods and Winter Storage.

"Mmm? What you say?"

"You're going, aren't you?"

"Haven't thought about it."

"Yes, you have. You were humming. I don't understand. I simply don't understand you. You've got a novel to finish by February. You've got work promised out everywhere. You're working fifteen hours a day and you look *awful*. And in the middle of it you're going to drop everything and go off to stupid North whatever it is..."

"Portage."

"...and you'll come back even more tired and crazy and who has to put up with your foul temper? Eh? Who has to take care of you if you get sick? And it won't be long," she said, "before the first hard frost."

"It's a marvel to me," he said, "how you *know* these things."

"And the back yard needs digging and the..."

"*You*," he said, "*you're* the one who's saying I'm going somewhere. Have *I* said I'm going somewhere? *Have* I?"

"What about the storm windows?"

"What *about* the storm windows? Bugger the storm windows. I am *tired* of storm windows. What have storm windows to do with anything? Who *mentioned* storm windows? It's like living in a lunatic asylum. Eat your cheese."

"I'm telling you now," she said, "novel or no novel, I am not doing the storm windows again myself."

"Good. Splendid. Three cheers for you. We're all agreed. So don't say it again. Don't say the words 'storm windows'."

"But *why*? I still don't understand *why*."

"Why *what*?"

"You just can't afford the time. You've got four more chapters to write. And then you've got rewriting. Why go to some ridiculous..."

"Sheila!"

"...to read to half a dozen..."

"*Sheila*!"

"...semi-literates who've probably never read any of your ..."

"ENOUGH! YOU ARE DRIVING ME INSANE! LEAVE ME ALONE! I am sitting here quietly and peaceably, meditating on this and that, bothering no one, TRYING TO EAT MY BLOODY BREAKFAST. IS IT TOO MUCH TO ASK THAT YOU REFRAIN FROM..."

"*Yes!*" she said.

He set down his cup.

"*Yes!*" she said. "*Wazoo-wazoo! Yes!*"

She met his stare, her colour high.

"I hope," she said, "that you're feeling proud of yourself."

"'Wazoo'?" he repeated.

"Poor Pogo," she said, "is trembling."

He uttered what he would have described as a broken cry.

With large, melodramatic gesture, he placed the back of one hand limp against his brow and clapped his other hand over his heart.

"Oh, sweet, injured womanhood!" he cried. "Oh, the quiet dignity with which she bears her pain! Oh, pathos insupportable! My eyes! My eyes! They start with contrite tears!"

Bending and sticking his head under the table, he said in a squeaky voice, "Diddums rough, brutal male raise his voicey-woicey? Who's going to the SPCA? Who's getting the purple needle-weedle? Absolutely painless. *Yes!*"

"*Yes,*" said Sheila patting Pogo, "*yes. Bad* Rob."

"It's pretending, you silly cow. It's too retarded to be frightened."

"Who's a *bad* Rob?"

"Only yesterday," he said, "that neurasthenic rug you're cuddling savaged the hose on the oil truck."

"*Big* wag-wags!" said Sheila.

"Right through to pink rubber."

"She's *terrified* of you," said Sheila.

"She isn't terrified of the oil man."

"*Yes!*" said Sheila. "Uzz a *good* girl."

"Uzz a bad actor," he said.

"*Not* an actor, is it, Pogo?"

"All it wants is your cheese."

He lighted another cigarette.

She looked pointedly at the stubs in the ashtray.

"You haven't answered my question," she said. "You're *refusing* to answer, aren't you?"

"The second you've gone," he said, "that allegedly terrorized animal will be asking me for a Triscuit."

"Why *are* you avoiding this?"

"Terrified!" he said. "Even *squirrels* like me. They come up to me in the park."

"I'm asking," she said, "because I'd really like to know."

"Very well," he said with a sigh. "All right. If that's the way you want it. You ask why it is possible that I might go to North Portage. Firstly, then. Speaking, of course, purely hypothetically. Firstly, my dear Sheila, *were* I to go, the Canada Council would pay me the sum of two hundred dollars. Derisory as that may be, it still represents two hundred *more* dollars than the coffers presently..."

"We're all right for a while," said Sheila.

"We are? Bring on the champagne. This must be the first time in the long history of our connubial association."

"And maybe you'll get some royalties in or something."

He sighed loudly and theatrically.

"'Or something'," he repeated.

He smiled at her with hideous sweetness.

"You've never quite grasped the royalty situation, have you? I think it *means* something to you it doesn't mean to me. In your *mind*, I mean. Perhaps it's the word itself. Royalty. Riches. Some kind of primitive word-magic."

She folded her arms.

"Royalties, Sheila, are the percentage of the list price I receive on copies sold. Thus, were a book of mine to list at ten dollars, I would receive for each copy sold the sum of one dollar. The only flaw in this arrangement, Sheila, the sole drawback, the one fly, as it were, in the literary ointment, is that not many copies of my books are sold. When we use the word 'royalties', we are, in my case, talking about such staggering sums as two hundred dollars. You *know* this. You have known this for all the years of our married life. Yet you *persist* in talking of royalties as though it meant an armoured truck pulling up to the front door. This aforementioned..."

"All I *meant*..."

"*Please.* This aforementioned munificence arrives twice a year. The next royalty payment is due in February. In February, it is distinctly possible that I will receive a cheque for one hundred dollars. The problem, Sheila, the problem *is* that it is now September."

"Oh, I *know*, Rob, I *know* how you feel but there's no *need* to..."

"Pay, however, no attention to these four leanish months. Or is it five? *One hundred dollars!* On what shall we spend this embarrassment of riches, my lambkin, my little lambchop? Throw a bone in the direction of the Mastercharge card? Blow it on a down payment for a bag of Mixed Party Nuts?"

"But there's no *need* for you to squander your time," said Sheila. "We've got enough between us to get by."

"Enough what? Kraft Dinners?"

"There's nothing *wrong* with..."

"I'd noticed the cupboard was bulging with familiar blue packages. *And*, of course, the sardines. Even the dog cringes now. All you've got to do is show it the can and it tries to get behind the settee."

"It's *you*," said Sheila. "If you'd..."

"I am inured, Sheila, to Managers' Specials of the Week. I have not spoken out against Partially Thawed Bargains. But I draw the line, the line is drawn, at No Name Brand sardines in unspecified oil."

"I suppose *you'd* like to live on smoked salmon and capers."

"Yes," he said.

"But really, Rob. If we're careful..."

"With brown bread and butter. And lemon juice."

"But I'm serious. If we..."

"You think I'm *not* serious? With *real* lemon juice. Not that reconstituted filth from the fridge. That stuff in the green bottle you're always buying."

"If you'd only make a few economies," she said. "Like not taking your shirts to the cleaners and..."

"Oh, no need to remind me that you're doing the bread-winning and I'm properly grateful and I certainly don't want to bore you with sordid domestic tales but I must confess, Sheila, that I do sometimes feel that while you're ensconced in your government office you're insulated from life's harsher realities. What few economies I might possibly make would be as a drop in the proverbial. *You* don't have to stay at home all day fielding abrasive calls from Bell Telephone's Miss Fiddes. *You* don't have to suffer the importunities of Yves' Plumbing and Heating. You're spared the whining of the Assistant Manager of the Bank of Nova Scotia, R. C. Matthews B. Comm. Not to mention..."

"You *haven't!*" she said. "You haven't been *buying* things again!"

"Buying things?"

"*Have* you?"

"Other than lashing out on a tube of Crest, I haven't..."

"It's not rare books, is it?"

"Is *what*? Trying to follow your mental processes," he said, "is like...is like attempting to lower a live eel tail-first into a condom."

He paused, struck by what he had said.

Condom?

He gestured dismissively.

"However. Much more important than money is the *idea* of the thing."

"What thing?"

"The idea," he said, "the idea that there's this tiny town somewhere up there. Remote. Isolated from everything that's going on. God knows what they do up there. Lumber, let's say.

Fishing. Mining something, maybe. There's one main street and then it's sprawled everywhere. Two or three of the buildings are Victorian stone—the town hall, maybe a bank with turrets—but the rest are all frame. All anyhow. And there are two new mini-plazas each with concrete-block supermarkets —one at each end of the town—and a *vast* liquor store and a Brewers' Retail. And there are ten churches representing every denomination you've ever heard of plus a couple you haven't—shacks with spires where nightmare families from the back roads speak in tongues.

"You're getting this?

"Can you see this place?

"What else? What else is there?

"There's a pizza joint run by a Greek and a Builder's Supplies yard and a weird store that sells Royal Doulton figurines and tartan scarves in cellophane boxes. Next to that there's Dolores: Modern Hair Stylings. And then there's the Re-Lax Restaurant, red plastic booths with individual juke-box selectors, Chinese and Canadian Cuisine. All the food's with red sauce and canned pineapple and there's a big Molson Beer clock and calendars of Chinese cuties from that plum-sauce sachet distributor in Montreal.

"Ho?

"Hum?

"Wing?

"Are you with me?

"And everyone drives pick-up trucks that blast out eight-track tapes of country-and-western all-time favourites and everyone wears workboots and plaid shirts and men are men and women are grateful. And the men who don't wear work-boots have their hair permed curly and nylon shirts you can see pink through.

"Oh, and there's a Legion Hall and a curling rink and a Masonic Lodge above a live-bait-cum-groceries store that sells hunting licences and a woman who runs the Sears Catalogue on the premises of Victory Billiards where the Voyageur bus stops. And a staggering amount of alcoholic adultery.

"And in the midst of all this desolation there's a small group —you see, it doesn't *matter* how many—there's a small group who feel there's a bit more to life than whooping it up on skidoos with a thermos of ready-mixed Harvey Wallbangers.

"So there they are gathered together in an upper room above Berman's Dry Goods and Winter Storage. *Who* are they? *I* don't know. How do *I* know? It might be the young reporter from the *North Portage Intelligencer and Weekly Record* and a couple of middle-aged women who'd taken piano lessons when they were girls and the volunteer lady with the collapsing hair who administers the library-loan system on Tuesday and Thursday evenings and can never figure out the date-stamp. Who else? The obese young man, say, who works in the family hardware store on the main street and has tendencies. Maybe even some gentle, leftover hippie who's into honey and stained glass. A couple of kids, perhaps, from the Regional High School. Misfits. They've picked it up from *somewhere*. Oh! Lawrence, say. Or Brautigan. Vonnegut, maybe. Who *knows* what they read! Not from the school library, *that's* for sure, because that's got enough books to fill a cupboard and they're all tattered *Star Trek* paperbacks and Judy Blume and *Conan the Barbarian*.

"Now I'm not saying I'm the Messiah—this isn't a *personal* thing at all—but one of them's read something of mine. Maybe just only *heard* of me. So there they are and it's the end of their Thursday Evening and they're wondering if he'd come to read, to talk, to be in touch with them, to put *them* in touch with...well, whatever it is they imagine goes on in the larger world.

"Maybe they *are* a bit dim, some of them, and they haven't read enough and their tastes are unformed—I grant you all that—but they're *trying*, they're groping towards something. And that's not a bad kind of audience. Not for anyone. And this is frankly sentimental but maybe there's *one* there—one of those high school kids—he doesn't *say* much—just stares a lot

and goes red—but he's *listening* and maybe years down the road
we'll hear from him.

"It's not so impossible.

"Is it?

"Can't you see what I'm trying to say? I *owe* things, Sheila.
I've got some kind of responsibility, some kind of *obligation*.
No, not so much to them as individuals but...it's really diffi-
cult not to sound pompous...but I'm a writer and I want writ-
ing to go on. Not just *my* stuff. But readers, reading, books.
The whole thing. The tradition, I suppose you'd have to say.
Does that make sense? I don't know. Perhaps not."

He shrugged.

"But I think so. I think it does."

He shrugged again.

Turned up his palm.

"How *could* I turn them down?"

In the silence, he lighted another cigarette, blew out a
stream of smoke, shook the matchstick with strong flicks of his
wrist, dropped it into the ashtray.

Sheila was watching him across the breakfast table.

He cleared his throat.

"It's a long time," she said, "since I've heard *so much* bull-
shit. Even from you. *Sickening*!"

He raised his eyebrows.

"This vision of you anguishing over the young man from the
hardware store and the bright kid from the high school. *Sickening*! You don't anguish over your own two, do you? You won't
even say good morning to them."

He closed his eyes and shook his head.

"Every time," she said, "every single time you've come back
from reading or lecturing, what have I heard? I've heard how
much you've hated it. How you're never ever going to do it
again. I've heard about their inane questions, their spots, their
inability to read. That's what *I've* heard."

"Oh, for God's sake! That's just bad temper. I'm usually
tired when I get back, that's all."

"Yes," she said, "and *I* know why. Because you've been drinking yourself stupid till all hours of the night and chasing after arty-farty *shiksas*."

"That is flatly untrue."

"I've *seen* them. I've seen them *looking* at you while you're up there performing and being charming. I've watched all those sluts with their hair and their caftans and their hand-woven sweaty ponchos and their leather boots up to their necks and their disgusting *thighs*."

"Sheila! For God's sake, don't start!"

"Oh, I know I'm not intellectual," she said, "and I'm not arty and sensitive but at least..."

"Enough, Sheila! Come on! Enough."

"Please do not interrupt me, Robert. I was about to say that although I might not have all the attractions of your would-be-artistic admirers, you do have to admit that *I* do not come home *diseased*."

"I refuse," he said, "I absolutely *refuse* to go through all this *again*."

"I'm not surprised."

"Yes, it *did* happen just after I got back from a reading but you know perfectly well that that was pure coincidence."

"Pure's what I'm not so sure about."

"Why are you *doing* this? You *know* there was no question of disease. You came with me to the doctor's. You *heard* what he said. It was a genital sore only in as much as it was on the genitals. *There is a profound medical difference between herpes and a cold sore.* What I had is what some people get on their lips."

Sheila nodded slowly.

"In winter," he added.

She continued staring at him.

"Yes," she said. "But yours just happened to be on your little *petzel*."

He closed his eyes and breathed.

"In the summer," she added.

He placed his clenched fist against his forehead.

"Which wouldn't have happened if you'd kept it in your pants. And now, if you'll excuse me, I have to go and put my make-up on."

She dropped the rumpled newspaper onto her chair.

"Or should that be 'put on my make-up'?"

He listened to the scuff of her slippers along the passage and the *creak-creak* of the first two steps of the stairs.

He shuffled together his mail piling it on top of the large manila envelope.

His head was throbbing.

His breath escaped him in a great audible groan.

Pogo's tail thumped the legs of Sheila's chair.

"*No!*" he said. "*Bad* dog!"

F orde's nerves were crying out for alcohol.

Though resigned to the necessity of aircraft, he remained entirely unconvinced of their safety. He regarded drinking before boarding a plane and while on it as a sensible health-precaution. Hours of tension and anxious sobriety could easily induce the heart attack he knew was waiting for him. For a relatively modest sum, he could remain benignly plastered until decanted at the other end. It was his habit to drink as much as was consonant with not actually weaving on arrival.

The flight to North Portage on Tributary Air had left him shaken.

The plane had seated sixteen and had propellers and little black wheels like the balsa-wood models his sons used to make. It was noisy inside and bits of it seemed to vibrate at different speeds and rhythms. The pilot had entered the plane from the rear after the passengers were seated; his shoes needed polishing; his paunch was considerable. A man with a cowboy hat on and long sideburns had called to him: *Hey there, Dick, they give you your licence back, eh?*

The stewardess.

Passengers called her Cindy.

She had been wearing a strange one-piece uniform that suggested more than anything else the practice garb of a martial art.

He had not at first been able to grasp the full significance of her question.

She had asked him if he'd like shortbread cookies or cheese and biscuits with his Coke or ginger ale.

And now *this* ménage.

Nodded again.

Made agreeing noises.

"Well, I'm aware that this might not *sound* useful," he said to Martin Prunes, who in his struggles with the plastic lid had managed to get his thumb in the Almond Chicken Guy Ding, "but it's a question of rewriting and keeping *on* rewriting until…"

"No more grown-up talking!" said Natasha.

"*Until,*" he repeated loudly, glancing at this hateful child, "one has…"

"Oh, *no!*" said Mrs. Prunes, groping in the brown bag. "Don't *tell* me!"

"Are we missing…?"

"Ah! *There* it is! Now, if Mr. Forde'll just for a minute…"

"The…?"

"…while I get Natasha's…"

She plopped into his hand a stapled wax-paper bag of steamed rice.

"And, please," he said, smiling, "let us not stand on ceremony."

"No feet on tables, Natasha," she said. "Pardon?"

"Rob," he said.

Arm in the brown bag, she looked at him.

"Ceremony," he repeated.

Paused.

"Lack of," he said. "Most people call me Rob."

The four of them were sitting on the floor around an old dining-room table that had had its legs sawn off and had been painted electric blue. Martin Prunes was sitting yogi-like, his sneakers wedged against his thighs. The disposition of Mrs. Prunes's legs was hidden beneath the floor-length and voluminous cotton dress.

Forde shifted from ham to ham.

The bag of rice, warm and heavy, had conformed itself to his palm; it was growing warmer; he had no idea *why* she wished him to hold it; it felt as he imagined an aged breast might feel.

"Rob, rob, rob, rob, rob," said Natasha.

"Just keep on until...?" prompted Martin Prunes.

"Pardon? Oh! Yes. Until one *knows* that one—"

"I want," said Natasha, rapping on the table with her spoon, "no more of this talking among grown-ups!"

Forde raised his eyes to the milk churn. Behind the child's head, it blocked most of the window. From it drooped bedraggled pampas grass. The churn had been painted over with aluminum paint.

Rust was blooming through again.

"Are we," he said, making the slightest gesture with the bag of rice, "going to be using...plates?"

He and Prunes had just returned in Prunes's wrecked Volkswagen from a restaurant whose only visible sign had read: Chinese Food and Gas. The home cooking promised in the letter had not materialized because—he'd now heard 'Mara' and 'Mora' and just possibly 'Moira'—because Mara or whatever had been working all day on posters for the Pro-Choice Campaign, a preoccupation Forde, having met Natasha, could well understand.

Who was busying herself flicking all the bits of green pepper from a carton of unidentifiable noodle and goo.

"Oh, yes! Yes, indeed!" he said as Mrs. Prunes steadied with both hands over his tumbler the magnum of Spanish screwtop.

"But..." said Prunes.

Forde listened, nodding judiciously. Declining Mrs. Prunes's offer of camomile tea, he drank the wine as quickly as was decent while Prunes's discourse stumbled on and, as if rapt, reached out and refilled the glass. It was large even for a tumbler; it said Coca-Cola on it in red and black; he remembered that such glasses had been a bargain offer some years earlier at McDonald's; even three-quarters full, it held a more than satisfactory amount. Behind Prunes's bushy hair and in front of the bricked-in fireplace stood two bicycles. Was the wine, he wondered, *really* causing his gums to pucker? The last of the evening light was glancing off handlebars and rims.

"But," said Prunes doggedly, "what if I *know* it's right, it's, like you said, it suddenly has that *feel*—but it isn't *really* right? Because what we're talking about here, well, that's essentially a subjective judgement. Isn't it?"

Forde did more grave nodding.

He looked up at the Ansel Adams poster—boulders and things—as if for inspiration.

"Well, it *is* and it *isn't*. It's a question of *time*, you see. A question of experience. Over a period of time, the *quality* of your knowledge—yes, that's a good way of putting it—the quality and *reliability* of your knowledge deepen, you see, the more you write and..."

"This," said Natasha, "is getting ridiculous."

"Have some won-tons," said Mrs. Prunes, "before they get cold."

"Mucous," said Natasha.

Forde crunched.

Natasha began to clonk together the wooden soles of her mother's discarded clog-like shoes.

"No more talking among grown-ups," she said, "and let's all do something creative."

"It's too near bedtime," said Forde.

"No it isn't," said Natasha.

Forde swilled wine.

"I know it isn't bedtime," she said, "because I know how to tell time and it isn't even *close* to bedtime because I know when bedtime is."

"Hmmmm," said Forde.

"Katya's got a cold and she's still even *in* bed."

"It's that time of year," said Forde.

"Are you old?" she said. "As old as my grandfather?"

"I don't know," said Forde. "Probably not quite as old."

She considered him.

"I saw a pigeon drop down dead," she said.

Forde leaned his weight on his other hand. His palm was corrugated from the carpet. The milk churn with its drooping pampas grass was becoming a dark shape. His buttocks were numb.

Mrs. Prunes began gathering debris.

Martin Prunes had withdrawn into a rude brooding. Reaching with thumb and forefinger into the slit-pocket of the vest he was wearing over a plaid shirt—a vest which once had been part of a dark, formal suit of antique cut—he brought out and started unrolling and rolling up a strip of celluloid. It looked like a length of 16-mm film or a bit of an Ikea tape-measure. Emanating from him was an inexplicable sullenness.

"My panties," said Natasha, who'd been busy creating a glutinous design on the table-top with strands of noodle, "have got a Strawberry Shortcake picture on them and I think that's extremely silly, don't you?"

"Really?"

"Mr. Forde?" said Mrs. Prunes, proffering a congealing aluminum dish.

He smiled, sketching a curving stomach, and shook his head.

"*And*," said Natasha, "I sleep in a double bed."

"Me, too," he said.

"But it's with my sister."

"That's nice," he said. "So you don't get lonely. How old is she—your sister?"

"It *isn't* nice," said Natasha, "and when I'm six, I'm going to have a bed of my own."

"Oh, good," said Forde.

"She's always making the bed shake," said Natasha, "and

keeping me awake *and* waking me up."

"Perhaps she's dreaming," said Forde.

"Oh, no," said Natasha, selecting and placing another noodle, "she's *always* masturbating."

Forde raised his tumbler and studied it; he pursed his lips as if considering the aesthetic aspects of the Coca-Cola calligraphy.

"But when you say," said Martin Prunes suddenly, "'over a period of time', how long does it..."

"Who'll finish up this last egg-roll?" said Mrs. Prunes.

Forde patted his pockets for cigarettes and lighter.

"How long, you mean," he said, "before one's knowledge becomes reliable? Mmmm! Well..."

"*Arrghhh!*" shouted Natasha. "Oh, *gross*! Look what he's doing! He's *smoking*! *Arrghhhh!*"

She started to work up a forced, racked coughing. The strain of this brought on dry retching. Breath whooping, she gibbered.

That she knew the term 'sidestream smoke' did not surprise him.

"Oh, Tasha!" wailed Mrs. Prunes. "Angel?"

The child was becoming interestingly mottled.

"HOW ABOUT," bellowed Forde, arresting the paroxysm, "IF I FINISH this in the bathroom?"

He left a silence behind him.

The stairs creaked and groaned. The Prunes family occupied the top two floors of the old house which was gloomy with small leaded windows, dark panelling, and heavy, dark trim. A damp wailing was coming from a room with a closed door. He slid home the bolt on the bathroom door and sat on the edge of the tub.

Beside the toilet was a blue plastic potty, imperfectly cleansed.

Much of the peeling enamel was covered by damp-bulged Harvey Edwards photographic posters, those posters one saw in stores in every shopping centre. Tattered ballet slippers.

The neck of a violin and tensed fingers. Leg warmers with a hole in one of them.

Over the tub, a poster-sized reproduction faded to a soft grey of a solid, naked lady.

He stood for a moment tracing his fingertips over the chipped and layered paint on the old radiator. It reminded him of home, of the radiator in his room just beyond the further edge of his desk, the way the paint on the wall behind the radiator ended a ragged brush-length down, and below that the archeological colours of earlier inhabitants.

Something *about* that photograph over the tub...He turned and looked at it again. Meaty; thyroid eyes staring at the camera; hair down to her buttocks; smudgy pubic bush. It was badly faded, possibly a Xerox enlargement. It looked...*ethnographic*. Photograph from an early British Museum handbook on the Oceanic collections. Daughter of the Headman. Village Maiden. Cult Devotee.

He leaned in over the tub.

It was, he realized, Mrs. Prunes.

The shrill wailing of Natasha's sister was developing a nasty edge.

It was his inevitable luck that Martin Prunes had published a story. He had been presented with a copy of it. Though it could have been worse; it might well have been poems. He no longer made any attempt to keep up with the mushrooming literary magazines. *This* thing was stapled and printed on hairy paper. It was called *Orca: A Magazine of the Northern Experience*.

He flicked ash into the grimed wash-basin.

Mickey Mouse toothbrush. Pluto toothbrush.

The brushes of the big Pruneses.

Into the mirror, he made garrotted faces, eyes crossing, tongue protruded, his pontificating voice echoing inside his head boring him anew.

They seemed to merge, these young and aspiring writers. There was something about them, something slightly hostile, grudging, something…it was as if they were in some odd way contemptuous.

Advice?

He let his face relax.

Stared at himself.

You *really* want advice about being a writer, kid?

The *real* McCoy?

He leaned closer to the mirror.

Get your hedgebackwards hair cut. Shoes, boy, leather, shined. Shirts, white. Postdate this, kite that. Beg, borrow, steal.

Establish credit.

Kiss academic ass. Get an agent.

Give serious consideration to desertion.

Matrons, Martin, like their writers *clean*. Matrons buy books. Matrons dispense sandwiches, small sums of money, and, on rare occasions, alcohol. Attention, then, to fingernails. Trim nasal hair. Let me speak frankly, Martin. Burn the vest. And, not to be personal, but just a word about the entertainment of distinguished literary guests…Though near-poverty will doubtless be your portion, drinking wine from jelly-jars and fast-food glasses is not only aesthetically repellent but…

This isn't a *game*, Martin.

It goes on.

This is not a game.

The mirror was fogging.

He was startled to realize he was whispering.

In the loft above Berman's Dry Goods and Winter Storage aged election posters for the Progressive Conservative Party plastered the walls. Clyde Willard, Clyde Willard, Clyde Willard, a bald domed head in blue. Light glanced off the empty metal folding chairs. Behind the eleven members of the North Portage Thursday Evening rows of metal chairs stretched back towards the shapes of stacked cartons. The loft smelled of warm lumber. The red eye on the coffee-urn glowed. He was aware as he was reading of the three dress-maker's mannequins; they were standing near the urn; he had to resist turning to them. Whenever he raised his eyes from the typed page to pause, to emphasize, to gesture, he saw hanging from the central rafters five links of a paper-chain, a withered balloon, a wasp's nest.

He slowed into the last paragraph. Dropping his voice, pulling the tiny audience closer to him, spinning out the lines, he wrapped them in its rhetoric. He allowed the silence to extend for a few seconds before closing the folder.

He inclined his head again and smiled.

The clapping was enthusiastic.

As he was squaring the sheets of manuscript, Martin Prunes rose to offer oddly formal thanks; *he was sure that they would all wish to join with him in expressing*, etc. Sundry announcements followed: coffee; copies of the latest issue of *Orca* available at a discount; the fast-approaching registration deadline for the Poetry North Workshop. He concluded by reminding the North Portage Thursday Evening that the following week Eric's presentation was to be a critical appreciation on tape of the life of Elvis Presley.

Forde accepted from a middle-aged lady in a bowling jacket and high heels a Styrofoam cup and a stir-stick.

"I just wanted to thank you," she said, "for a very enjoyable presentation."

"Thank you very much," said Forde.

"Did I hear a British accent?"

"Probably," said Forde. "I guess you must have done."

He smiled.

"My father was from the old country," she said. "From County Devon."

"Ah!" said Forde.

She smiled.

"Barnstaple?" she said.

Slowly shaking his head, Forde said,

"It was a long time ago."

During this conversation, Forde had been uncomfortably aware of a man's face on his left behind his shoulder and very close. He turned to meet eyes magnified to an horrific degree.

"I was wondering," said this man, "if you know the name of a nature book I once read?"

Forde smiled tentatively.

"I've forgotten the name of it and the author," said the man, "but it was about otters."

Forde could feel his eyes beginning to water.

"Otters," he repeated.

"Yes," said the man.

He was darkly unshaven.

Forde started to shake his head.

"He's written other books as well," said the man.

"No," said Forde, "I can't at the moment recall..."

"The cover's a photograph."

"I'm sorry," said Forde. "No, I'm afraid..."

"Green and blue, mainly," said the man.

Forde shook his head.

The man continued staring at him.

"I don't suppose," he said, "you've had much chance to see the lake yet."

"Only from the air."

The silent, swimmy stare compelled him to add:

"Unfortunately."

He cleared his throat.

"You'll notice," said the man, "a lot of dead fish in it."

"Really?"

"Pollution's one of my interests."

"Sugar," said Forde, "if you'll excuse me just for a moment..."

Beside the urn, a plump, florid man in a greenish suit was agitating the surface of his coffee with a stir-stick attempting to sink the coffee-whitener which had spread over it in a yellowish scum.

"...but what a difference," said this plump man to the

young man with the pony-tail and the combat boots, "after switching to that soluble 18-5-10."

"Chris was telling me," said the pony-tail youth, "that slugs have been chewing the shit out of him."

"Mia Prinex, the silly boy," said the plump man, "that's the answer to his woes."

Pasted to the soiled canvas torso of the middle mannequin was a tourism sticker bearing the provincial flag and the words: *Ontario—yours to discover!*

"It is Ottawa, isn't it?" said the myopic man who'd suddenly materialized again at very close quarters.

"Pardon?"

"Where you live? Ottawa?"

"Yes," said Forde.

"I was wondering," said the myopic man, "if you'd sighted any peregrine falcons?"

"No," said Forde.

What Forde needed was drink. He was tired yet charged from the reading. It was something he was familiar with. He could feel it within himself like a ground swell in the blood, massive and distending, flooding energy which would counter until late into the night the day's exertion and fatigue. Even when that tide was ebbing and he lay red-eyed with exhaustion in hotel rooms, motel rooms, rooms in motor courts, guest bedrooms, its pull still stirred him, kept him wakeful, a barge half-sunk at its moorings, slow, sullen water slop-slopping in the hold.

The only antidote was drink. Insecticides, lateral feeding, bone meal—behind him the horticultural entrancements bore on. He glanced at his watch. No one seemed to be making moves to leave. If he were to sleep, he needed drink in generous measure.

"Chris got under glass—what was it?—the *second* week in August?" said the pony-tail youth.

"*Mea culpa*," said the plump man. "I admit it. You were all quite right. I was sorely remiss. But all's well that ends well."

Forde picked up the jar of coffee-whitener and studied the label.

It said:

Predominantly of Vegetable Origin.

Although he had no burning desire to talk to anyone, he felt put out that no one seemed to want to talk to *him*. People had stared, had nodded.

Wide, splintery floor-boards, election posters, rows of metal chairs.

He stood holding the Styrofoam cup.

Prunes, whose unspoken duty it was to purvey alcohol, was gabbing away to a woman near the door. The myopic man was now peering earnestly up at Prunes with his mouth open; the seat of his pants was baggy; his face was creased and lined, the skin strangely coarse and grainy, something he'd noticed before in retarded people...difficult to judge how old he was.

Forty?

Possibly younger.

Forde imagined him cared for at home by aged parents. He had a big mug for his tea with a picture on it. Niagara Falls, perhaps. He had a special egg-cup shaped like a rooster and a special spoon. An apostle spoon? Commemorative? Of what? The Coronation! Big blue handkerchiefs with white dots on them. He sucked cough-lozenges. Extra-Strong mints. Winter and summer over his shoes he wore ungainly rubbers. Carried his library books in a net nylon shopping bag. Often had a plug of absorbent cotton in one ear. A pocket-watch on a chain attached to his lapel. There was something about his belt, dark brown, wide, the clasp circular...what *was* that?...something tantalizingly familiar...*yes*—it would be a Boy Scout belt bunching his shapeless flannels. He attended auctions, lectures at the library, haunted United Church Bake Sales, Baptist Jumbles, Anglican Rummages, his change in a woman's change-purse or in one of those horseshoe-shaped leather purses, coins counted carefully out...

"Mr. Forde?"

He was startled.

"Larry Portby," said the plump man. "I teach English and Creative Writing at CSH."

"How do you do?"

"I have a confession to make."

"Oh? What's that? Sounds intriguing."

"I enjoyed your reading."

Forde looked at him.

Portby smiled.

"I know the name, of course," he said, "but I have to admit that I've never read anything of yours before."

"You're in a majority," said Forde.

"Pressure of *time* and..."

Forde, who had heard this and its variants often, nodded.

Portby shrugged.

"...and so on and so forth. Joe, here—"

"How do you do?" said Forde to the youth with the pony-tail.

Joe gave a reluctant nod.

"Joe and I are discussing pumpkins."

"They're re-establishing themselves in the Ottawa area," said the myopic man suddenly.

Portby turned around to look at him.

"Because of the pigeons."

"What are?"

"Peregrine falcons."

"Oh, *fuck*!" said Joe.

The myopic man blinked and frowned.

"Pumpkins," said Portby. "The subject of our discourse, Henry, is pumpkins. We are talking about pumpkins. You are probably unaware," he said, turning to Forde, "that you are addressing the man who has the honour of being President of the North Portage and Environs Annual Great Canadian Pumpkin Fest."

Forde raised an eyebrow.

Portby sketched a bow.

"As President," he said, "I find myself in the pleasantly

embarrassing position of being one of this year's serious con-
tenders for the Grand Prize. I lie awake at night wondering
what to award myself."

"Not so fuckin' fast, Kawolski," said Joe.

"Oh, ye of *little* faith!" said Portby.

He laughed.

"No, Chris Simpson and I—he's where you're staying
tonight—Chris and I are locked in a deadly end-game, as it
were. Our lives seem to have become devoted to coaxing and
cajoling the beasts. They're not here tonight, by the way—
Chris and Vinnie—they're off down the lake closing up the
family cottage. Perhaps you've come across the name? Simpson? I mention it because he's had things recently in *Orca* and
Quarry and that magazine from Alberta...name escapes me.
It's a pity you're going to miss him. Young Christopher's
something of a protégé of mine. He is, in my humble opinion,
a very promising young writer. And Joe, of course, Joe here's a
published poet."

"Aw, shit, eh?" said Joe.

"It's a small group that forgathers," said Portby, "and we
may, perhaps, lack some of that sophistication to be found in
more southern metropoli but..."

"Excuse me, Larry," said Martin Prunes. "What we usually
do is take people round to the hotel for a few beers if that's..."

"Fine," said Forde.

"You can send out for pizza if you..."

"Beer sounds marvellous," said Forde.

"With any fuckin' luck," said Joe, "we can catch the last
quarter."

Martin Prunes unplugged the coffee-urn.

A woman clattered metal chairs.

A drift towards the door began.

"So these pumpkins," said Forde, "the glass is to get them
bigger, is it?"

"Oh, fuck, man!" said Joe.

Forde glanced at him, at his ankh on a thong.

"Pardon?"

"This isn't fuckin' Toronto!"

"No," said Forde.

"No," said Portby, holding open the door while Prunes brought up the rearguard with the keys. "I think Joe's referring to the disadvantage under which we labour up here. If we didn't, we couldn't produce them at all. A late spring and a fall much earlier than yours, you see. Our growing season's very short."

They followed the others down the booming linoleum stairs.

On the sidewalk, it was suddenly cold.

Forde and Prunes waited as Portby set down his briefcase, an elaborately strapped and buckled affair in soft leather. The footsteps of the others who were walking on ahead echoed in the deserted street.

"Well," said Prunes, while Portby was inserting himself into a strange Bavarian-looking loden overcoat, "that was an experience. Really."

"Thank you," said Forde. "Thank you very much."

"Where the rhythm of it changed," said Prunes, "I picked up on *that*, but I'm not so sure if I followed, you know, intellectually..."

"But there's nothing intellectual to follow," said Forde, watching Portby hurling about himself the ends of a long collegiate scarf. "It's all simply emotional, all simply a question of *language* and..."

"Ah bitter chill it was!" said Portby.

"Sorry...?" said Prunes.

"The owl," said Portby, settling his hat, "for all his feathers, was a-cold."

"This..." said Forde, "this *notion* of yours that..."

"*Avanti!*" cried Portby.

He raised his stubby, telescoped umbrella like a baton.

"Rhetoric!" said Forde. "Getting the rhetoric right, that's what it's about. Think of it as, oh...as stringing a necklace, say. *Words*. You try this against that. Watch the way that changes this. Take care of that," he said, gesturing, "and you'll find ideas've taken care of themselves. See what I mean? I mean, in that piece I was reading…"

"Of course," said Portby, "there was obviously a strong element of humour and playfulness about the whole thing."

"Humour and *playfulness?*" said Forde.

"At the beginning," said Portby.

"*Humour?*" said Forde.

"But in some odd way," said Portby, "things changed. I've even gone out at night in pyjamas to commune with mine."

Forde raised his eyes to the War Memorial.

"They seem to do something to you," said Portby. "I'm at a loss to account for it and this may sound fanciful and rather science fiction but there they sit getting bigger and bigger and they seem to *draw one to them*. I know that sounds crazy but there they…well…*are*—orange and huge and sort of…"

His stubby umbrella described large, slow circles.

"…sort of *implacable*. Anyway, mystical or not, it's developed into an event of no little importance among the group of us, this plumping, as it were, of the swelling gourd and………

P leasantly awash with beer at someone else's expense, Forde gazed out of the Volkswagen's windows incuriously. They were passing again the War Memorial and the granite horse-trough. Prunes had turned the heater on. Warmth washing his legs, Forde felt, he decided, good. The traffic light was suspended on wires above the centre of the street; it seemed to glow with a peculiar intensity.

After the traffic light, modified bush began. A few widely separated concrete-block buildings. Texaco Station. EATS. Place with a crane.

Leading off the black tarmac, the pale openings of dirt roads, the mouths of dirt and gravel drives, tin mailboxes on cedar posts.

He shifted in the seat.

Pollution, pumpkins, pizza with pineapple, pissed poets—nothing about the evening had surprised him; it had unfolded like countless others over the years; it had been an evening, he thought, *typically* peculiar.

He found himself hearing again the voice of the woman in high heels and the bowling jacket; in a cartouche on the sleeve, 'Freddie'; across the back, 'Marston Seed and Feed'.

My father was from the old country. From County Devon.

Ah!

Barnstaple?

It was a long time ago.

The noise of the hammering engine seemed to fill the car.

He never had been to Barnstaple; it was Salcombe he remembered. He'd spent a farewell week there with his closest friend from university—was it twenty years ago?—a beery week of sailing mishaps, of frantic ragworm-digging at low tide, of slow hours fishing for flounder and dab. He thought back, calculating. Nearer to thirty years ago, he realized, those days that now seemed always sunlit, days of overdrafts and sausages. Hilda? Could that have been it? The name suggested itself. Those lovely long fingers. The teller at the Broad Street branch, the student branch of Barclay's, who cashed his small cheques without checking his balance. Until he'd been summoned beyond the raised flap in the counter and ushered into the sanctorum of Major Grey.

'What possible explanation can we offer for this...for these...umm. *Mmm?*'

The intricate mechanism inside the glass door of the brass carriage clock on the desk twirling, twinkling, checking, twiddling back.

'You *thought* you had sufficient money in your account? *Thought*! And what would become of us all if we simply *thought* things? Mmm?'

Holding his Parker pen with the fingertips of both hands beneath his narrow grey moustache. Maroon. Silver cap. Rolling the barrel of the pen over his moustache up to touch the underneath of his nose, down again.

'*Mmm?*'

Turning the pen until the silver arrow of its clip was correctly positioned to enable him to stir and scratch upwards with it the bristles of his moustache.

'Surely you must realize, Mr. Forde, such...well...*extraordinary...*'

He waved a hand over the cheques spread on the desk.

'...utterly *cavalier...*'

Rasp.

'...but of *honour...*'

Rasp.

'... simply *isn't banking!*'

The university year finished, only a week had remained before he sailed from Liverpool; he'd needed money to sustain his novel in those weeks in Canada before the start of his September job. On his way out of the bank, he'd written a cheque for one hundred and fifty non-existent pounds, nodding and saying to the lavender harridan,

'I've just come from Major Grey.'

He wondered what had happened to that manuscript. He'd made quite sure it hadn't gone to the University of Calgary with his other early papers. It was years since he remembered seeing it. He hoped it was safely lost. He could remember what it looked and felt like, the heft of it and the perished rubber of the two red elastics, but he could scarcely recall what it had all been about. He wondered what it had been he'd thought so important. What had been so important to him at the age of twenty to have caused him to suffer through the labour of a book? What could he have imagined he'd *known?* Though he suspected it had been less a question of subject matter that had driven him than of desire, the longing to *be* a writer, the desire to be numbered in that glorious company. Sheets slightly smaller than quarto, holes punched for a three-ring binder—he could see the manuscript clearly. What *had* it been about? He had some memory of a scene involving a religious maniac and a goat.

The heat was making him drowsy.

He shifted in the seat again.

Opening out, a vista of the lake.

Tourist Cabins.

NIGHTCRAWLERS.

Though the beer had, in another sense, been dearly bought. He had had to endure further baroque instalments of Portby's pumpkins past and present, Prunes's tedious enthusiasms for writers who embraced and expressed social and political philosophies, Joe's surly attacks on him as a representative of the literary Establishment centred in the decadence of the South, and arabesques from Henry on the subject of DDT.

'Establishment'.

The very concept caused him some bitter amusement.

His drifting thoughts lodged for a moment on a review from the very centre of that southern sophistication and sybaritism, a review in the Ottawa *Citizen* of his twelfth and most recent novel, a review whose cheery vulgarity and mindlessness still filled him with rage and shame. It had opened:

Grab the suntan lotion, a sixpack, and the latest by Ourtown's Robert Forde and head out for the beach...

He grunted.

"Pardon?" said Prunes.

He glanced across at Prunes's profile, the thin, serious face, the bushy hair, glint of light on granny glasses.

Slowly, he shook his head.

"Grapple them to thy soul, Martin," he said, "with hoops of steel."

"Pardon? What?"

"*Not* ideas," he said, waving his hand in a dismissive gesture. "*Words*."

Prunes nodded.

"Martin," said Forde, rousing himself, "I have decided to share this with you."

"What?"

"And I wouldn't with everyone."

"Share what?"

"I have decided to tell you a story, Martin. A story of sudden and unsought bounty. In Ottawa the other day, for reasons I won't go into, I had to buy a new tie. As a matter of fact, *this* tie."

"They're just down here," said Prunes, "on the edge of the lake. It's an old house that's been turned into apartments."

The car turned off onto gravel.

"*This* tie," repeated Forde. "So. There I was, then, strolling about clothes stores. Couldn't find a single thing. And then I went into one of those places that call themselves 'clothiers'— you know the sort of thing. All the assistants in dark suits and generally sort of *hushed*. Sort of places that pretend they were there when whatshisname disembarked. The explorer chap. Cartier. Long wooden counter with an inlaid brass rule. Bolts of cloth lying about. *Mahogany*, know what I mean? Anyway, I didn't like anything this clothier character was showing me and he said,

"'Have you given thought to something in pure silk?'

"So out came the boxes of ties in pure silk and I found one I did like and do you know what he said? You don't. You *couldn't*. I felt like dragging him across his counter and raining down kisses on his upturned moustache. What had happened, you see, was that I'd discarded some of the silk ties and made another pile of possibles but *both* piles were silk. That's important. Right? So..."

The car seemed to hit something, stopped with a jolt.

The headlights were burning onto railroad tracks. Beyond them were sere bulrushes, trunks of trees. The tracks were rusted dark orange. Fallen now from their height, withered by the frosts, rank grasses had grown up between the ties, milkweed with gaping pods, brown and ochre husks.

"Well," said Prunes, "here we are."

It was cold outside the car and silent. The stars were bright in an immense sky and, looking up, Forde began to feel dizzy.

"Over this way," said Prunes.

Gravel crunched underfoot.

Forde stood holding his small suitcase.

Keys, stairs, a door.

"Anyway," said Forde, "there I was with the two piles of silk ties in front of me and..."

"Excuse me," said Prunes, reaching round him to switch on lights. Facing them was a narrow kitchen like a galley. They were in a passageway.

"Will you be all right?" said Prunes.

"Sure. Fine. Anyway..."

"And I'll be over in the morning," said Prunes, "for breakfast and the airport and everything."

"Thank you. So..."

"That's the bedroom there. And Vinnie left towels and..."

"Listen!" said Forde.

"Look, er, Rob. It's getting late, so if you don't mind I'd better head back. I'll see you in the morning. About eight?"

Forde stood at the open door listening to the sounds of his going. The Volkswagen roared. He stood there for a few moments and then shrugged. Closed the door and attached the chain with the knob on it into the sliding thing.

He stood in the passage.

The silk glinting under the lights above the counter.

Holding up draped over his fingers the two ties of his final choice.

Ah, said the assistant, returning after a discreet absence, *I see the preference, sir, is for silk with a slub.*

In the apartment's heavy silence, Forde said:

"Slub."

He walked down the passage and into the sitting room.

He bowed to his reflection in the window's blackness.

Struck an oratorical pose.

Said:

"SLUB!"

Sinking back into the couch, he looked around the room. He felt as if the long hours of being polite and affable had bulged the flesh of his face into the wooden grotesquery of a ventriloquist's dummy. For several minutes, he just sat. In the strange silence, he seemed to hear somewhere in the room the sound of something electric, the faintest suggestion of sound, the tense soundless sound of an open phone line, but the only place it could have been coming from was the stereo equipment and he could see no lights. He put his feet up on the tile-topped coffee table, spread his arms along the back of the couch. It was difficult to believe that it was over—not to be with someone, not to be listening, not to be talking.

He widened his eyes and slowly rotated his head while mechanically opening and closing his mouth.

On the coffee table stood a cactus plant in a little green plastic tub. It was in what he supposed would have to be called flower. Its green, ridged shaft was topped by a bulbous head, red and pitted. It looked like the glans of an ancient penis in the terminal stage of a loathsome disease.

He untied his shoe laces and eased off the shoes. His feet were swollen. He tried to think of what that part of the foot was called, the part right at the top of the shoe's tongue where the laces tied. 'Bridge'? The bridge of the foot? Somehow, it didn't sound right. He wiggled his toes. Regarded his stocking feet. Sighted through the V they made and fired a few rounds of H.E. shells at the padded head-rest strapped to the rocking chair.

Sheila had said that the puffiness was just something that happened as you got older, imperfect circulation or some such, but he was convinced that it was flying that did it, unnatural pressures, Tributary teetotal bloody Air. He wondered if these sodding Simpsons had anything to drink.

In the fridge, there was an opened can of Alpo covered with aluminum foil, a cabbage, and a packet of Cow Brand baking soda. He opened cupboards. There were the dregs of some foul liqueur and an unopened bottle of brandy, Greek but it would have to do.

"Needs must," he remarked to the ceramic cheeseboard as he poured a healthy snort into a glass that had white daisies on it.

Glass in hand, he wandered from room to room.

The bathroom was unornamented. On the wide window-ledge lay a branch of antler-like driftwood, the tines hung with necklaces and earrings. The necklaces were all plastic poppers with big beads. Plastic bangles. A pair of Navajo-ish earrings. There was nothing fascinating in the cabinet. Topical ointment, a resinous roach-clip, Contac-C, Aspirins.

He shook out three and washed them down with the brandy, shuddering. Useful for countering hangovers before they arrived and according to an article he'd read somewhere had the effect of thinning the blood or some such thing, important, apparently, in case of heart attack.

The bed had bright red sheets on it. He poked it. It was a water bed. He pushed it. Sat on it. Bounced. He had never slept on one before. It seemed unpleasantly responsive to movement. Its interior tides, he thought, might well reduce love-making to a desperate rodeo.

In the kitchen, he topped up the brandy. Garlic on a string. A pan with a copper bottom. Stained copies of *The Joy of Cooking* and *Uncle John's Book of Bread* and *Recipes for a Small Planet*. In a net bag under the sink, sprouting onions.

Fixed to the fridge door with a magnet, a file card that said:
I.O.U. $25.00
C. Simpson.

He stood staring at this card, considering its possible implications. He took if off the fridge to see if anything were written on the back.

Wandering back into the sitting room, he stood looking about him. Two sides of it were uncurtained glass, something about the room suggesting that at one time it had been a sunporch. Stereo equipment with buttons and dials like a jet plane's cockpit. Records in a red plastic milk-crate. He crouched to look at the paperbacks in the bookcase. Most seemed concerned with 'women's issues', a term he had always considered unfortunate.

Sisterhood Is Powerful. The Well of Loneliness. Orlando. Rubyfruit Jungle.

Outsize books by Women's Collectives.

Hystera: An American Feminist Quarterly.

Flipped through the pages. His attention was held by an advertisement at the back placed by the Lunar Press in Berkeley soliciting for an anthology personal stories of convent life by lesbian former nuns.

On the top of the bookcase there were two pieces of fan coral, a conch, a slobbered Hartz Mountain rawhide 'Chewy' bone, and a plastic cube with photographs in it. One was a wedding photograph, presumably of these Simpsons. They looked absurdly young. More and more, people were looking younger and younger. Who was it who'd said that you knew you were getting older when *policemen* started looking young?

E. M. Forster, perhaps?

Though *he'd* had a specialized interest in looking at policemen.

Poor old bugger.

He sat down on the couch with the plastic cube.

He drank more of the brandy.

He examined again the photo of what he took to be Vinnie; she didn't look stuff tough enough to spread alarm and despondency among the troops but he kept thinking of Prunes's letter—'the person with whom he lives'; it sounded as though she had them all walking on eggshells. The other photographs were of a monstrous black dog with a lolloping tongue the size of a salami, a mom, a dad who looked a bit like Lenin, a car, a cottage.

In the kitchen, the fridge shuddered into silence.

He tried the rocking chair; it was uncomfortable.

He got up.

He watched it rock.

He'd been given on the plane a plastic package containing something called 'Cheese Food'; sealed inside were two crackers and a plastic stick for getting it out; he had put it on the floor. The stewardess had been called...Cindy.

He scribbled in the tiny notebook he always carried.

The note above said:

sign on a hotdog stand—EVC Food Systems.

That was one Sheila would enjoy; he made a mental note to tell her.

At the airport, tears welling into her eyes as they always did when they said goodbyes, the delicate pale-violet skin beneath her eyes puffy and darkening as if bruised, making her look older, vulnerable.

What *was* he doing?

Why *had* he come to North Portage?

He had, of course, lied to her. It wasn't really the money. It wasn't any sense of responsibility to the bright kid from the high school or the obese young man from the hardware store, she'd been quite right. Nor was it marked devotion to that more abstract kite he'd flown, the waning tradition of literature.

Why *had* he abandoned work on his book to come to this one-horse dump? This one-horse-trough necropolis? To end up in this apartment's empty stillness?

He'd once thought of such jaunts as 'building an audience'; he no longer suffered from that delusion.

Was it, he wondered, simply a need to escape, a paid holiday, a chance to remind himself that a world existed beyond the world of his white, facing wall and the shadowy spear-shaped markings of the grain in his desk-top?

Or could it be that he'd become addicted to performance itself, to the surging power of adrenalin? Addicted to the subsequent unfettered drinking?

'Unfettered drinking!'

Five beers or whatever it was and two glasses of nasty brandy. He stared at the diseased cactus. What a desperado he was! What a Roaring Boy!

He grunted aloud at his own nonsense.

He sat turning the plastic cube.

Or was it simple vanity? He knew himself greedy for praise and flattery. He admitted it. It was not a pleasant trait. He had to constrain himself at parties.

'I'll look for it in the library.'

'Will it be coming out in paperback?'

'And do you write under your own name?'

When these people at parties told him how much they were looking forward to his next, murderous pressure throbbed behind his eyeballs. 'Next'! There was something wrong with the last? You didn't like the preceding ten? *'Next'*! As though his books were effortless as bowel movements, their agonized production as assured as the next morning's newspaper.

When they told him how much they'd enjoyed his last, he smiled and thanked them but inwardly howled:

'Enjoyed it', did you? Filled in a few odd moments for you, did it? Moments snatched from feeding your fat face or humping this frump of a wife. 'Enjoyed' it, did you? This isn't Agatha bloody Christie on a wet afternoon we're smiling about, you mindless rat's ass, THIS IS MY HEART'S BLOOD.

Yet greedy as he was for praise and susceptible as he was to the grossest flattery, he had not flown here for that; what a sad ego would have been inflated by *this* night's audience.

So was it, then, something more contorted, darker, some weakness more deeply hidden? Could it be that he needed to confirm again for himself by contact with an audience, *any* audience, even *this* audience, that he was indeed a writer? That he did indeed *exist* beyond that facing wall, that desk-top? Were excursions such as these to confirm that he was indeed Robert Forde, receiver of Awards, subject of exegesis, the eminent Forde who occupied four columns in the *Oxford Companion to Canadian Literature*? Was *that* what it was all about?

Was the smallness of his audience *still* undermining his sense of purpose? Was the solitude *still* eating at him? Was the general indifference *still* sapping his strength? Was he, after all these years, still so weak, so pathetically insecure, that he *need-ed* to parade himself in North bloody Portage?

He feared it might be so.

He set down the plastic cube.

He feared such might be the case.

Though it was possible he was just flagellating himself because he was feeling guilty about Sheila. Yawning, he stood and stretched. Or, equally possible, the answer was:

Other.

None of these.

Taking with him the saucer he was using as an ashtray, he wandered into the bedroom. The light shade was made of yellowed parchment; the bulb was of low wattage. There was no lock or handle on the door, just a hole where a handle had once fitted; he pushed the door to. On top of the chest of drawers stood a triple mirror framed in bamboo; in the room's yellow, soupy light, he examined his reflections.

"What amazing preservation," he remarked aloud, "in a man of forty-nine."

He was careful with his suit pants over the sliding, rounded chair-back. There was no blanket. There were no blankets in the drawers. It was so chilly that he decided to sleep in his shirt. Sitting on the edge of the bed, he pulled off his socks; they had patterned his feet with lines. Bent, he studied them. Then, switching off the light, he cautiously got himself into the drunken bed. Its movements were decidedly unpleasant; more viscous than liquid, it made him think of cold molasses, creeping porridge, Channel crossings. He shivered beneath the single sheet.

He lay on his back in the darkness listening to his breathing.

He wondered if Sheila *really* believed him at this moment knee-deep in a moist poetess or stretched, spent, over a heta-comb of aspirant novelists in leather boots.

She had few doubts about his motivations. She'd once said he was monstrous, a swollen child...

Smiling in the dark, he pictured her...

Arseface.

...scenes and rememberings of that dreadful morning running through his mind...

In his study with the door slammed shut, he sat at his desk staring at the blank wall facing him. The room's chaotic filth, its perilous stacks of books, its piled papers, the caked ashtray with its pyramid of butts, the wicker wastepaper basket overflowing onto the floor—all this brought him some little comfort.

The warped door of their bathroom forcing into the frame.

Water roaring in the antique plumbing.

He glanced listlessly at the top sheet of the loathsome stuff he'd written the day before. He hadn't the heart for it. He signed his name a few times on a file card. Doodled. Crossed off the date on his calendar.

Footsteps overhead.

Rattle of wire coat-hangers on the chrome bar in the closet.

Straightening out a paper-clip, he started to clean his fingernails.

Footsteps.

The creak of the top stair.

He got up and opened his door.

"Although you may not choose to believe it," he said, looking up at her, "I have been faithful to you..."

"Excuse me."

She brushed past him on the narrow landing.

To her descending back, he said,

"...ever since the day of our marriage. You ill-mannered cow."

Leaning over the banisters, he called,

"I have adored you for twenty years!"

Clack of her heels along the passage.

Closet.

Coat.

Clack-clack coming back.

Looking down at her from his position half-way up the stairs, he said,

"I have been as faithful to you, Sheila, as...Christ!...as a *metronome!*"

As she opened the inner door, she said, "Tock-tock. Tock-tock. Is that it? You're trying to say I'm boring?"

"*No!* You're fucking *impossible!*"

He glared at her, tapping his forehead.

"You know what? You're not just weird. You're clinically

potty. I'm beginning to think you need seeing to."

Red-faced from bending and zipping her boots, she straightened up holding her purse and a plastic bag from the Ontario Fruit Market with her shoes in it and said in a hollow voice,

"Ha. Ha."

"I beg your pardon?"

"It was *you*," she said. "It was *you* that needed seeing to. And what a fool you looked coming back out into that waiting room with your fly gaping open!"

The door slamming shut behind her.

The stained-glass cornucopia-things rattling in their leaded panels.

The wire basket beneath the mail slot falling off and skittering on the tiles to bounce and lodge on a boot.

Cautiously, Forde essayed a turn. The bed lurched and then swayed back under his head. His foot extended into a new area of coldness. He knew that even if he managed to fall asleep, the cold would wake him at some black, unchristian hour. Sighing his reluctance, he eased himself out of the bed and straightened the sheet. Over the sheet he spread his towel. In a closet in the passage he found two raincoats, a denim jacket, and what looked like a nurse's cape. He spread these on the bed. Over them, he draped and arranged the rug from the bedroom floor.

Inserting himself beneath this swaying weight, he lay motionless. Gradually, the mounting warmth unclenched, released him, and his drifting thoughts homed back to the events of that earlier day, to Sheila.

He saw himself at his desk.

The day destroyed, he had sat there, moody, brooding, sulky, until a possibility of rearrangement in what he'd written the day before snagged his attention. It was an obstinate scene, recalcitrant, the timing hopelessly *wrong*, a conversation set in a Chinese restaurant where the incomprehensible waiter's recommendations and queries were constant interruptions to Arthur's tortuous declaration of passion.

Taking his special red marker, he began to draw arrows of rearrangement which suddenly released the whole knotted mess. Before he'd known what was happening, he was writing fluently, stuff flowing so fast he could scarcely keep up with it, shorthand squiggles, positions of paragraphs blocked in with a few words of suggestion. He'd written until lunchtime oblivious to the stirrings of his sons, the eruption of stereos, kitchen clatter, the doorbell, and the door's repeated slammings. He had eaten something for lunch. Standing over the kitchen sink. Bread and something.

When exhaustion forced him to rest, he was in high good humour. The next day of rewriting was solidly in his grasp. The boys had disappeared; he cleared away their mess. He prepared a chicken casserole, the kitchen warm with the smell of *pancetta* and onions, sharp with the rising fumes of the vermouth. Peeled potatoes and parboiled them to add to it later. The stalks of her broccoli were yellowing and woody; doubtless a Manager's Special. He doused this dubious vegetable in salt water to extrude the caterpillars—a refinement she often forwent. Turned on the gas at full blast under the dregs of the morning's coffee.

On days when his writing went well, he rewarded himself with treats. On this day, he had polished his brown shoes—a peculiarly soothing activity, the smell of Kiwi, deep into the welts with the old toothbrush, the soft brush bringing up the shine until they glowed with a range of honey colours that always reminded him very precisely of dates.

And then he had indulged himself in a long, meticulous shave, foam unstinted, a new blade.

He had surveyed her morning wreckage with feelings of the deepest affection and delight.

Rattle of wire coat-hangers on the chrome bar in the closet.

Out across the bedroom the morning trail of indecision, clothes draped over the chair, dropped on the floor, slung on the bed: too tight, too blue, unironed, too warm, too old.

In front of him, soiled tissues, the capless toothpaste

squeezed in the middle, oozing, the wash-basin spattered with diminishing spots of watered-down blue eye-liner where she'd flicked the brush. Beside the basin, the muddle of pretty pots, the cakes of make-up in compacts, blue and purple, rouge, rose and madder, conjuring for him the black enamel tins of Reeves watercolour paints from the mornings of birthdays long ago.

And among the clutter on the counter-top, among the tubes and pots and creams, the cuticle scissors, the tweezers, the brushes, a tube of Preparation H; she applied it to the lines and creases at the corners of her eyes.

Arseface.

The hour or so between the time he finished work and her homecoming were the longest hours of his day. His exhaustion always surprised him. He was too weary even to read. Usually he sat nursing mugs of tea, waiting.

He had heard the front door closing, the thump of her boots coming off, the rustle of paper bags.

"Forde?"

'Forde' was his professional self. She'd picked it up originally from reviews and articles, Forde this, Forde's that, and she'd used it as a deflationary joke, but after a time he'd heard her on the phone to friends saying quite unselfconsciously: 'Not this weekend. Sorry. Forde's working.'

Used directly, however, 'Forde' had somehow become an endearment.

"Hello?"

"Forde?"

They'd sat chatting before dinner and sipping Scotch. He retailed the day's bout with the landlord and Yves' Plumbing and Heating, both now attempting in collusion to claim the thermostat in perfect working order. Sheila entertained him with gossip about the alphabet of characters in her office. Marilyn, the fluffy scy i who had abortions like most people had fillings, was off again to Montreal. This time she thought conception had occurred because she wasn't expecting it with George while they'd been looking round an Open House.

"What do you *mean?*"

Sheila shrugged.

"But...*where?*"

"In the powder room."

"You see! You're *deliberately* leaving bits out."

Dinner passed peacefully. Chris was, as usual, tranced by food. Tony had not returned; Chris said he thought he'd gone to see the Home Hardware girl. Forde managed a diplomatic amount of broccoli. Casually, Sheila'd asked him if he'd got much written and he'd thought for a moment of describing a day laid waste just to make her feel worse but had been unable to contain his restaurant.

"Vintage Forde, missee. Especially this waiter. I *love* my waiter. Everything he says is a declarative sentence. Even questions. And he's abnormally *loud.* Also incomprehensible, of course. And he laughs a lot. It's quite unnerving. Anyway, you'll see when I've worked on it a bit more. But as scenes in Chinese restaurants go, it's number-one-son. It would not be going too far to say, Christopher, my child, that it is a many-splendoured thing."

Blankly, Christopher had passed the salt.

After dinner, they suffered his latest attempt from memory at the life-cycle and general doings of wolverines.

Honourable judges, Mrs. Grecci, fellow-students: the title of my speech is: Nature's Savage...

When, with much prompting, he had stumbled through, he said he had to work on his project.

"Pardon? On *what?*"

"Pasta."

"What do you *mean*—'pasta'?"

"Different kinds of pasta."

Forde lay on the couch watching Sheila read. From the kitchen, the sluice and thrub of the dishwasher. The stereo pulsing from Chris's room upstairs.

He watched the almost imperceptible agitation of a frond of the false aralia in the warm air rising from the radiator.

He said:

"You can go off wolverines, can't you?"

"Mmmm."

"What *are* they? I mean, what do they look like?"

"They're a fur-bearing mammal," said Sheila without looking up, "of northern habitat but considerable range."

For some minutes, Forde studied the cornice where the
ornate plasterwork was darkened and cracked; for reasons
obscure even to him it suggested caries.

He said:

"They were at home today."

"Mmm?"

"The boys."

"Mmmm."

"Why was that?"

"I *told* you. It was a P. D. Day at school."

"Oh."

He cleared his throat.

She lowered the book and said,

"Aren't you working tonight?"

"No. Not tonight. I don't think so."

In certain lights, the fronds of the false aralia looked like
metal. Sometimes like wrought-iron, sometimes bronze. Like
the ancient patinated bronze of the ritual vessels in the Royal
Ontario's Chinese collection.

Turning his head and looking across at her, he said,

"What did he *mean*—'pasta'? He's nearly *thirteen* for
Christ's sake!"

"Shss."

He yawned audibly and elaborately.

She closed the book.

"You're always randy when we've had an argument,
aren't you?"

"Am I? I mean, yes."

"Do you think Tony's got his key?"

"Yes, *yes*."

He is holding out his hand. He is pulling her up out of the

chair. She is laughing. She makes a noisy kiss on his nose. They are standing with their arms around each other.

"It's just," she says, "I don't like it when you go away."

"I know."

"You just can't *afford* to squander your time."

"Mmmm."

"No, I don't mean just the book. I don't mean just February. I mean..."

"I know."

He is kissing her chin, nuzzling into the side of her neck.

"I know what you mean."

Forde's head pushed into the pillow. His swaying covers rose into a hump over his shoulder. In the warmth beneath the towel, the denim jacket, the raincoats, the cape, and the carpet, Forde uttered a long, loosening sigh. His breathing thickened, his body shuddering towards sleep.

He lay looking at the rectangle of the window seeing it as it would be when winter set in, opaque, milky with a climbing crescent of ice. He no longer dreamed of wealth and fame; he dreamed of warmth, of a house warm enough not to wear sweaters in, of bathrooms like the bathrooms in magazines, bathrooms bathed in rosy warmth from overhead heating devices of the utmost modernity.

The sound of a toothbrush dropped back in the porcelain beaker.

He turned his head on the pillow.

It was cool in the bedroom. The ruby numerals on the digital clock glowed in the dark, and seemed to float. The closed door of the bathroom leaked light around its frame. The hot water was running. The sound of the cupboard door beneath the basin opening.

Down both sides of the frame and along the top where the warped door did not properly close, soft light radiated. The diffuse glow suggested the depths and gradations of the old moulding on the door's outer jambs, hinted on the brass of the door knob.

He lay looking at the brightness of the light beneath the

door. He could see under the door onto the white tiles, see on the tiles a faint, stationary reflection. He could see along the line of light on the white tiles the sudden shadows of her movements.

The sound of the cupboard door again.

He lay watching the play of shadow, the linen sheet teasing the heat of his body with its weight and touch.

He felt he could feel its very weave.

Woken early by his feet freezing beyond the raincoats, he had found himself—it was in the flesh of his neck, the hollow of his throat, on and in the hair on his chest—it was everywhere—he had found himself *covered in fine grit.* No soap in the bathroom, he had showered using instead the Simpsons' shampoo, a herbal concoction called Elfin, and now smelled all over faintly like cough medicine. Seated opposite Prunes in the airport's concession restaurant, The Jolly Chef, and surrounded by the North Portage Seniors, a girls' volley-ball team three-quarters of them inexplicably Chinese, Forde felt his morning rage and irritation deepening into something approaching anguish. His knuckles gleamed in a white grip on his cigarette lighter as he watched the slow approach of the coffee-pot.

"What?"

Prunes was persisting.

Forde shrugged.

"But what about Lessing? What would you say about Sartre?"

"Ah! Yes! *God*, yes!" said Forde, turning the cup the right way up. "And poached eggs with bacon, toast, and home-fries."

Years had passed since he'd tasted bacon in his own kitchen. Eggs had recently become restricted and begrudged. Butter had been banished. He was forced to water his beverages with skim milk.

He looked forward to the day when the cause of degenerative heart-disease was pinpointed as Crunchy Granola.

Forde considered it obvious to the meanest intelligence that the whole question of mornings and breakfasts was a medical question; the body on awakening was in a state of shock; it required immediate restoratives. The brain in the morning was being called upon to operate in a higher gear than it did during the hours of sleep but lacked the necessary fuel because it hadn't been fed for eight hours. Or more. Which was why he always ate a cheese sandwich immediately before retiring.

There was, perhaps, some slight *thickening* but it was untrue that he was overweight. He resented the way she tried to force saccharine so righteously upon him. *That* was what annoyed him; not the fact that she was flatly *wrong* but her insufferable, pissy manner. *She*, of course, denied that sugar *did* give one needed energy; carbohydrates, toast or some damn thing, he rarely listened. What did *she* know?

What was it that was administered to people suffering from shock? Was it toast? Was it Crunchy Granola? A nice bowl of spuds? It was not. It was, as everyone knew, a cup of tea. *Not*, she might note, a cup of tea with saccharine fizzing at the brim but a cup of tea so stiff with sugar you could stand a spoon in it. This was a medical fact. It could not be denied. What, pray, did she imagine it was that revivified and generally perked them up?

The hot water?

The milk?

The Orange Pekoe?

"...so I was thinking," said Prunes, turning to the grey, fraying, army-surplus bag beside him and flipping back the limp flap, "that you might..."

Forde steeled himself; he would plead pressure of work, deadlines, death in the family, the onset of glaucoma; he would *not*.

Sticking up from the bag was the manila envelope. The bag had sat between them in the Volkswagen. Forde had been aware of the manila envelope, top bent by the bag's flap, all the way out to the airport.

"...like to have these copies of our first three issues. The issue I gave you last night with my own, umm, thing, that's volume two, number one, but these have got two of Chris's stories and there's some of Joe's poems and..."

"Thank you."

Forde nodded.

"That's very thoughtful of you."

Prunes flopped the bag's flap down over the envelope again. Forde had set his face against it.

He held Prunes, if not responsible, then at least accountable for the lack of blankets and for the fact that he now smelled of cough medicine; he held Prunes responsible for the two and a half hours of waiting in the empty apartment without food or coffee, hours during which his digestive juices had probably made a start on the living flesh of the stomach wall, hours during which he'd smoked cigarettes until he'd thought he could quite easily vomit, hours during which he'd been reduced to reading an article in a fat book by a Women's Collective about the self-examination of breasts.

Even Prunes's *bag* irritated him.

If it hadn't been frayed army-surplus it would have been a leather satchel-like thing made of thick hide studded with copper rivets wrought by a craftsperson.

Politely, he turned a few pages—inevitable atrocious line drawings of nudes—and then put the copies of *Orca: A Magazine of the Northern Experience* on the seat beside him.

He looked around for the waitress.

Behind Prunes's bushy head, through the vast plate-glass windows, beyond the two runways where toy planes wavered down and disappeared on little wheels, there were purple hills covered with trees and snow.

Forde considered *his* response to the northern experience. Did they stay because they lacked the imagination to leave? The *normal* reaction to a place where the first frosts came in August would be to go to where they didn't. How could normal people deliberately choose to remain in a hinterland so drear that the *Globe and Mail* from the *previous day* did not penetrate until four-thirty in the afternoon? He was tired of manly men in tartan shirts who ate home-fries off the flat of their knives. And curling. And taverns with rock videos and aging stark-naked belly-dancers.

And trees.

"...and that's one of the things that's so fascinating about Chris's work. I mean, there's a story of his in there called 'Depositions' that's told from four different points of view simultaneously—it's all intercut accounts of the same event, you see, diary entries and the interrogator's reports and..."

"Interrogator?"

"Well, it's set in an unnamed country, you see, but..."

Christ!

Forde nodded from time to time.

Christ!

He had already had the gravest reservations about this Simpson.

As the large element on the stove had started to glow, pungent smoke had burned up for a few seconds. The Simpsons seemed not to have a kettle. He had put on a pan of water for coffee and opened the fridge for milk only to find himself staring at the cabbage, the opened can of Alpo, and the box of Cow Brand baking soda. It had not occurred to him the night before. He'd stood staring at the lighted emptiness.

In sudden panic, he'd yanked open cupboards, pushed aside jars, cans, bent and peered, herbs, stood on tiptoe, jars of dried flower-heads—*tansy?* The plastic tub labelled Sugar had contained nasty, mung-like beans. The coffee, when he'd found it, had been both instant and decaffeinated.

I.O.U. $25.00

C. Simpson

...in my pumpkin opinion, a young writer of great promise..."

It was inconceivable to Forde, who took pride in not having set foot in a shopping centre since May 1967, that a young writer of promise could wilfully drink decaffeinated dust. It seemed to him axiomatic that a man unsound on staples would be unsound on the semicolon.

Ballpark mustard in the cupboards, chemical gherkins, *instant* coffee, a brandy better left to Greeks—we are not quibbling about petty matters of taste, Simpson. What is at issue here is your sensibility. Snobbery? Privilege? Do you have the impertinence to suggest I'm merely advocating superior consumerism? Don't be denser, Simpson, than nature made you. It is *the whole man* who writes.

He had placed the shameful jar on the top of the fridge directly above the file card.

On the file card he had written in large capital letters:
NO!
BEANS, SIMPSON.
R.F.

"Ah! Bless you! And more coffee, please," said Forde to the waitress. And to Prunes, "Pardon?"

"I was wondering," said Prunes, "if you don't mind me asking, because I've been thinking about…well, whether you were able to live off your writing. Or do you have to do…other things?"

"I live," said Forde, "off the sweat of my frau. You are looking at a kept man."

"Oh, I didn't mean to…"

"Writers," said Forde, "are rarely embarrassed about money. Or lack of it. It's all they ever talk about. And with good reason. But…"

He gestured at his plate.

"Oh, sure," said Prunes. "You go ahead. Sorry. I'm just going to slide out and get some gum."

Chewing toast, Forde watched him as he threaded his way through the tables of volleyball nymphets towards the concourse where a woman in a sari was doodling at the floor with a broad mop. Tartan shirt coming adrift from his cord pants, down-filled vest over the leather lawman's vest, the long, thin cord legs ending in klutzy great yellow construction boots with red laces.

'Gum'.

Spreading the forbidden yolk, Forde brooded.

'Live off his writing'.

Christ!

Here he was.

Here he was on a jolly jaunt in North Portage that would earn him from the Canada Council two hundred dollars before tax, or, more realistically, one hundred and seventy before tax because even though he collected receipts religiously and claimed for every imaginable expense, money always seemed to melt away from him. Beyond this pittance, he had no money coming in that he knew of for several months.

Each of his novels earned him critical plaudits in the papers and pedestrian *explications* in subsidized journals and, on average, one thousand, five hundred dollars. He'd calculated once that this worked out to something like four dollars a day. The totally unskilled—positive *mouth-breathers*—received as the basic minimum wage close to four dollars *an hour*. This thought occurred to him with some bitterness whenever he read pissy articles about the burgeoning of Canadian culture.

He brooded about the Royal Bank, the Bank of Nova Scotia, and the Canadian Imperial Bank of Commerce—each of which had declined to issue him a Visa card.

He brooded about R. C. Matthews B. Comm.

About Managers' Specials.

About how *much* he disliked Partially Thawed New Zealand Bargains—soggy lamb gobbets Sheila got from a sort of bin at Loblaws.

He sometimes thought of his situation—and that of other writers he admired and loved—as being akin to that of a Victorian portrait painter who had refined his craft and art to a pitch of dazzling brilliance at exactly the moment that cheap photography had rendered him redundant.

Beloved of the granola-munching populace were books on cooking, dieting, exercising, investing, computing, the operation of wood-stoves, the clitoris, self-assertion, and World War II.

Six-figure sums were routinely advanced to *artistes* who penned swollen sagas of powerful industrial families, of immigrant families rising from poverty to become powerful industrialists, of landowning families who diversified into powerful new industries and became more powerful than they'd been before but at the same time becoming riven by incest, insanity, possession by the devil, litigation and Alzheimer's, homosexual and lesbian inversion, poltergeists and hysterectomy, losing that guiding vision of their founder old Grandfather Ebenezer who used to kneel on the good earth running soil through his wise old fingers saying wise dawn things to little barefoot Mattie who never forgot a single utterance...and who went on to found an empire in oil, microchips, and laser-beam technology before renouncing the world and establishing an Ecological Foundation and Nature Reserve in memory of Grandfather Ebenezer where she cleaned up oil-fouled seabirds and imparted gentle wisdom to little barefoot Bobbie who three hundred pages later would corner the world market in extruded protein.

Six-figure advances for this interchangeable fodder—not to mention the subsidiary rights for movies, TV, Talking Books, and T-shirts—six-figure *advances* for this silage all of which read as though the interchangeable authors were graduates in English as a second language.

While *he*, here he sat, half his lifetime spent labouring with words, no regular income and precious little *irregular* income, his fiftieth birthday approaching, here he sat in North Portage surrounded by female Chinese volleyball players armed with ghetto-blasters. Here he sat in North sodding Portage in The Jolly sodding Chef SMELLING ALL OVER OF COUGH MEDICINE.

Forde ground out his cigarette.

Ash got under his fingernail.

He sat looking at the tip of his forefinger.

Yet—undeniably—doubtless the sugar on its soothing rounds—he was feeling better than he'd felt before. Wires twisted to the point where at any second they might *spang*—

this relentless torsion of his nerves was slackening. He no longer thought it probable he might vomit; he had stopped gripping things; the inside of his head felt less like a berserk slot machine.

He stretched his arms, flexed the muscles in his shoulders.

On red, white, and blue ribbons round their necks, the North Portage Seniors were all wearing the gold-coloured medal of the Canada Fitness Award. Wired to a Sony Walkman and studying *People* magazine, the jock in the black tracksuit who was riding herd on them was joggling in his chair to private rhythms.

Forde again checked the time.

At the nearest table, two young men with beer-bellies and thick forearms were talking about moose.

Through the sliding glass doors that led out onto the concourse came Prunes again, lanky, gangling, the top half of him puffed out in his down vest like the Michelin man, the lower scarecrow half like Worzel Gummidge.

With angularity of knees, clumsy knockings of boots, Prunes worked himself back into the booth. He proffered an opened packet of Spearmint.

Forde raised a palm and shook his head.

"Why I was asking," said Prunes.

"Mmm?"

Forde looked up to find Prunes staring at him intently.

"About writing."

"Mmmm."

"About making a living from writing."

"Yes."

"Well, Chris's already decided to start teaching half-time next term to get more time to write."

"Oh," said Forde. "Mmm?"

Prunes started fiddling with the salt and pepper shakers.

"I read somewhere," he said, "that you used to teach once—was it high school?"

Forde nodded.

"So how did *you* do it?"

"Oh, you mean...well," said Forde, "God knows. It took a while. I wasn't married then. I'd built up bits and pieces, editing, bits of hack work, reviewing, bits for the CBC—that sort of thing."

He shrugged.

"God knows. Delivering phone books. I can't honestly remember a lot of it. Tutoring. This and that."

Prunes nodded slowly.

He started propelling the pepper pot with the salt shaker.

"You mean...?" said Forde.

"I know I want to write," said Prunes.

"But all this," said Forde, "was in Montreal."

Behind Prunes's head, a balsa-wood plane wobbled down and whizzled away on little wheels.

"It's a bit different."

Prunes nodded.

There was a silence.

"What about grants?" said Prunes.

"Well," said Forde, "yes, but you can't apply for a grant until you've had a book published. Can you? Isn't it the rule still? For junior grants, I mean?"

"Catch-22," said Prunes.

"It's not unfair," said Forde. "Is it?"

"It's the *time!*" said Prunes.

Forde nodded.

"But don't you think you're being just a little premature?" he said. "Thinking about this sort of thing right now? I mean, in terms of the amount you've got done?"

"All I know," said Prunes, "is that I want to write."

"But it'd make more sense to put a book together *first* and then..."

"That's what I do," said Prunes. "I *do* work. I drive myself every night. This is what my commitment is."

"Yes, but..."

"I don't expect it to be easy."

"But if you burned your boats at—CHS, is it?"

"CSH," said Prunes. "Collège Saint-Henri."

Forde sighed.

He shook his head slowly.

Prunes shrugged.

"I don't expect it to be easy," he said. "I'm not asking for that. Most writers have a hard time at the beginning. I know that. I'm not asking for that."

"I mean," said Forde, "if you were on your own..."

The silence extended.

Prunes started rearranging his arrangement of the sugar packets.

"The whole thing," said Forde, "the whole shape of this kind of life, it's all so...precarious. The turn of a card. Tails coming up instead of heads. There's often no justice in it—the shape of what happens. It all depends on so many things you can't control."

Forde spread his hands.

"And 'it'," he went on. "'It all depends...' What does 'it' mean?"

Prunes tore off the top of a packet of sugar.

"What 'it' means in Canada," said Forde, "is two thousand readers after twenty years."

Prunes poured the sugar into Forde's saucer in a rising mound.

"I'm sorry," said Forde.

He shook his head.

He took out a cigarette, lighted it, moved the ashtray closer.

"I *know* what you're asking me. I'm sorry. I can't give that kind of advice."

Prunes did not look up.

"How *can* I?"

The silence grew heavier.

Forde cleared his throat.

The man in the John Deere cap said that the worst fucking thing he'd ever smelled in his fucking life was a fucking moose when you gutted the fucker.

Over the loudspeakers sounded an announcement for Tributary Air; *pre-boarding* something *at this time* something *Ottawa proceed* somewhere.

"What was that?" said Forde. "Gate what?"

"There only is one," said Prunes.

The jock in the black track-suit rolled up his magazine and called,

"Okay, guys!"

"Well..." said Forde.

They walked together past the car-rental booth, past the Indian woman in the sari who was emptying ashtrays into a paper bag from Kentucky Fried Chicken, red laces in Prunes's big yellow boots, past a machine that sold insurance, past a glass case with a model airplane suspended inside it.

Forde stopped at the variety store to buy cigarettes. Standing at the cash, he glanced at the stand of paperbacks.

"Good God!" he said. "Look at this!"

There were Penguin books, travel books in the Picador series—an early Eric Newby he hadn't read—Pelican books on history and archeology, Naipaul, Narayan, Richard Yates, thrillers by Ross Macdonald, Ambler, Reginald Hill, James McClure, there were even a few books by Canadian writers.

"This is the best place in town," said Prunes. "The woman who owns it—her son was at university and he orders books from Toronto."

"Now she's *very* good," said Forde. "You ought to read this."

"This is where we all come," said Prunes.

The book in his hand, Forde turned and said,

"Pardon?"

"When the new selection comes."

"Sorry?"

"This is where we all come," said Prunes. "Everyone drives out here."

They walked on past the row of public telephones, past a sign saying that North Portage welcomed industry, past signs for taxis and the airport bus, a washroom for the disabled.

Standing by the sign that said

PASSENGERS ONLY BEYOND THIS POINT

Forde said,

"Well..."

And Prunes said,

"Well, on behalf of the Thursday Evening I'd like to express our ..."

"A pleasure," said Forde.

"...thanks to you and..."

"The pleasure was mine."

"It was an experience," said Prunes.

The lenses in his spectacles, caught at an angle of light, were spotty and smeared.

"Really."

"You know," said Forde, "I don't know if this'd be any use to you..."

Prunes stared.

Forde shrugged.

"...but if you'd like...if you feel...I could read over some of your things, make a few suggestions, perhaps, if that'd be...?"

As he walked out and across the runway, the last of the North Portage Seniors was framed in the plane's doorway. He was immensely pleased and relieved to get a double seat to himself. The stewardess took away his suitcase and put it somewhere in the front behind a curtain. On the empty seat beside him, he put his coat and the manila envelope.

After the take-off and the climb, the droning roar of the engines became almost hypnotic. Lulled by the plane's noisy progress, he stopped thinking about metal fatigue and death in slow motion in the endlessly tumbling debris and sat gazing out of the window at the hills and bare trees, his thoughts drifting over the events of the last twenty-four hours. Henry was presenting himself again. Forde was enchanted by his invention of Henry's Boy Scout belt. Taking out his notebook, he also gave him a hearing-aid, large, bulbous, a horribly wrong shade of pink.

A motel sign he'd seen from Prunes's Volkswagen:

Reception Room and Propane Gas.

Natasha in her tabard-like dress and Strawberry Shortcake panties.

Mara? Mora?—her arm in the brown bag.

Most writers have a hard time at the beginning. I know that.

He stared unseeing out of the window.

Nearly twenty-five years ago.

As long ago as that?

A small unlicensed restaurant in Montreal where he used to eat with other young writers when in funds. Italian. Below street-level. A dingy bespoke tailor above. He tried to remember its name. Grotto-like, the decor. Plaster stalactites and stalagmites inside niches cut into the walls, niches dimly illuminated with green and blue fairy lights. At about head-height, a frieze of shells cemented into the walls, scallop shells, oyster shells, shells shining with mother-of-pearl. The ceiling like stiff frosting on a cake.

A bowl of moules, the sauce mopped up with hunks of baguette, wine in teacups.

He could hear the roar of those hot, boastful evenings, the boundless energy of it, the optimism, the intensity of those arrogant literary friendships. He could taste the weird after-taste of that raw, fruity wine manufactured in Rosemount basements and garages. Those were the days he'd felt lordly in his poverty, the work beginning to appear in the golden magazines, *their* names beside the names that were known, magazines that now were long defunct, footnotes in unread works of reference.

He shifted in his seat, crossing his legs.

It wasn't the beginning that was hard.

It wasn't the beginning.

He put his notebook and pen on top of the manila envelope beside him; Sheila would be angry with him again.

The envelopes would arrive regularly. He would comment on the shapes of the stories. On this one, he would suggest cuts. On that, he would make a few comments about the woodenness of dialogue, suggesting a more systematic use of contractions. On another, he would select a few words here and there and query meaning or appropriateness; he would urge the use of a dictionary. On yet another, he would rework the opening paragraph, suggesting ways of getting more quickly into the life of the story. On this one, he would *again* write strictures concerning dialogue.

At first, the envelopes would arrive as often as every two weeks. Accompanying them would be long letters. After four or five months, they would arrive less frequently.

Then months would pass.

Down below, the meandering steel glint of a river. There a clearing. That straight line perhaps a logging road. As the plane bore southwards, the trees were beginning to take on colour, the last of the fall leaves.

Forde shifted in his seat again, sat back.

He stared at the back of the seat in front.

And then . . .

And then after long silence would arrive something with a scarcely legible signature, flamboyant scrawl, unfamiliar. Sheila and he would puzzle over it. What would that something be? A complimentary calendar. A catalogue. Something from the world of publishing. Printed under the difficult signature would be: Text-Book Division; or Associate Editor; or Trade Sales.

The company Christmas card, perhaps?